WELCOME TO THE FRIENDZONE

JESSICA GIRKE

Welcome to the Friendzone

First edition

Cover Design by AS Designs
Editing by Becky Clapham

Content Warnings:
Mental and physical violence
Death of loved ones
Child loss
Workplace relationship with power imbalance
Morally gray behavior (hiding forbidden love)
Mental Health Issues
Detailed sexual activities

Note

This novella has a lot of references to characters and storylines of the novel "Demons in your mind".
I would recommend reading DIYM first to get the full experience.

Welcome to the Friendzone

"You just gotta keep going and fighting for everything, and one day you'll get to where you want."
Naomi Osaka

Welcome to the Friendzone

This one is a huge THANK YOU to everyone who supported me so far. To everyone who wanted to know more about Marta and Oliver.
I wrote this novella for all of us.
For the ones that believe in love
and the ones that need a new book-boyfriend
to start believing again.

Welcome to the Friendzone

CHRISTMAS TRAGEDY

THEN

December 24th, 2018

"Frank?" Marta Gómez's voice echoed through the two-story house on the outskirts of Washington, D.C. She and her husband Frank had only moved in a few months ago, after house hunting for almost a year. As soon as Frank had parked the car on the driveway and Marta's eyes saw the dark wooden house with the white window frames and the old but beautiful white door with the round muntin window in it, she was in love.

"Yes, Baby?" Frank's calm voice came from the bathroom on the second floor.

He'd just returned from a run and was about to hop in the shower when Marta called for him. She loved the tenderness and tranquility of his voice. No matter how stressful life had been, he was there to calm her down, a characteristic that helped him greatly as a governmental lawyer.

"I'll drive to the supermarket real quick. We're out of butter and I wanted to bake some Christmas cookies for tomorrow," she said while jumping on one foot to get her other into her sneaker.

Her keychain danced along her chest as she held the end of it secured between her teeth.

"Okay, drive carefully! Remember, you're 70% responsible for the Peach." She could hear her husband chuckle before the sound of the shower was the only sound coming out of the bathroom.

The Peach.

Marta was 14 weeks pregnant, which meant the baby was the size of a peach right now. Because of her job as a CIA Agent in the drug trafficking task force, they'd needed to tell her boss and colleagues as soon as they'd found out, getting her out of immediate danger for the growing fetus inside of her.

Frank had been overprotective from the day they'd found out he was going to be a dad. They hadn't tried for a baby, the Peach a welcomed accident, but as soon as he realized that he wasn't able to do much more than bring Marta some comfort in the vulnerable first trimester he always joked that he was only 30% responsible for their child's safety, while Marta was taking on the rest. They hadn't told their families yet because they'd wanted to wait until they'd reached that magical 12 weeks.

At Christmas dinner the next day they were finally going to tell Frank's family the news of their growing family. That's why Marta wanted to bake cookies in the shape of baby onesies. She closed the freshly painted white door behind her, stepped towards her driveway, and into their car. The entire drive she bellowed the Christmas songs on the radio from the depths of her lungs, really feeling the vibe of this year's festivities.

It was the last Christmas she and Frank would spend alone.

This realization hit her as soon as she exited her car in the huge supermarket parking lot. It was decorated beautifully, full of sparkling lights, Christmas trees, and oversized candy canes. Instead of heading directly towards the ingredients she needed, she got distracted by the aisle that contained baby things. With tears brimming in her eyes and one hand covering her stomach as if she wanted to protect the Peach with her bare hand, she looked left and right until a beige onesie drew her attention. It had a fluffy teddy bear on the front and "Daddy's favorite teddy" printed right underneath it. Marta needed to swallow a few times to prevent the tears from falling. She grabbed the onesie and put it in her basket, sure that Frank would love it.

She took her time in the supermarket, wandering around the aisles without an actual goal, so it took her almost 40 minutes until she got everything she needed for the cookies. She made a quick check of her phone to see if Frank had texted her in case they needed anything additional, but no message was seen.

While waiting in line to pay for the stuff she had in her basket, she gently caressed her belly and mumbled to the child inside of it.

"Can't wait to show your daddy this super cute onesie. He'll freak out."

With an indestructible smile on her face, she entered her car again and made her way back home. It was a ten-minute drive that was again filled with loud singing and smooth dance moves behind the steering wheel.

It was already dark outside when she parked the car in the driveway. Their own Christmas decorations were still not lit and that bothered Marta. Normally, Frank was eager to turn them on as soon as the sun began to set. They could have easily gotten timer switches that would turn them on and off automatically but Frank had protested loudly when Marta suggested it. Turning on the Christmas lights was his favorite activity as soon as he came home from work. But today the lights were still off.

Without thinking too much about it, Marta carried her grocery bag towards their front door and fiddled with her keychain until she found the right key. Before she could turn it around in the lock to open the door she heard a loud crashing sound coming from inside their house.

Weird. What was Frank doing?

Just a second later she heard a gunshot, making her switch into Agent mode in the blink of an eye. With a swift movement she slid into the hallway after checking that nobody was inside. She knew she had a gun stored in the sideboard near the door, so she dug into the drawer and thankfully found the P99 pretty easily.

The house was silent. Too silent.

After the crashing sounds and the gunshot she expected to hear and see the intruders somewhere, but it was all quiet.

"Frank?" she asked up the stairs with a shaking voice.

No answer.

One step after another, the gun still in her hands, she climbed the stairs, securing the hallway before making her way to the bathroom. The last known location of her husband. The door stood ajar and with a gentle kick of her foot, she opened it. With her gun pointing around the room, she realized it was empty. No sign of Frank. Unlike a lot of houses, they didn't have the bathroom attached to the master bedroom, so she went into the hallway again and turned right. Their bedroom was right next to it, the door closed.

She listened carefully for any sounds coming from it before slowly turning the handle and opening the door. The light was on but she couldn't see Frank in this room either.

Then her eyes took in the crimson liquid that slowly made its way towards the door.

She gasped in shock the moment she realized that this was blood. A lot of blood. Lowering the gun, she stepped around their king-sized bed, and suddenly her heart stopped beating. Her brain stopped thinking. Her whole body shut down.

In the middle of a huge puddle of blood laid Frank.

Lifeless.

He was on his side, one arm in front of his face so that Marta couldn't see him properly. She also couldn't see where he was shot so she placed her gun on the bed and quickly knelt down next to him.

She didn't even feel the tears slipping out of her eyes.

"Frank? Frank?" She asked carefully before she tried turning his body around with one arm.

He was so heavy. Nobody truly realizes how heavy lifeless bodies actually are. With both hands and some more strength she finally managed to roll him onto his back. The angry wound on his chest caught her attention first. The blood was still oozing out of it.

"Oh my god." She inhaled sharply before checking his body for another wound.

It had been only one shot but she wanted to be sure. While digging with one hand in the pocket of her pants to grab her phone and call an ambulance she let her eyes wander along his body until they met his face.

Instinctively she knew what she was about to see.

That's why she avoided looking him in the face the moment she knelt down.

When she saw her husband's lifeless eyes a hot, burning blade of grief sliced into her heart, twisting around and going deeper with every beat.

The gray eyes that were filled with so many sparkles, affection, and adoration for her. The eyes that still showed her how much he loved her, even when they were fighting. The gray eyes she fell in love with when they first caught sight of each other in a meeting at the White House three years ago.

Those gray eyes were empty.

"Frank," she whined, trying to shake him back to life.

This couldn't be reality. This wasn't true. This was a dream. She would wake up soon, cry in Frank's arms, and tell him about the horrible nightmare she just had. She needed him. Peach needed him. She couldn't do this alone.

Suddenly she heard a noise from the walk-in closet behind her but before she could turn around to see where it came from a searing hot pain shot through her shoulder. She gasped loudly in shock, but finally managed to turn around.

She looked into the sneering face of a dark-haired man with a gun in his hand.

"You think you're undefeatable, Samantha?" He spat at her before continuing with a sharp voice. "Breaking news. We found you. Checkmate!"

Another shot left the man's gun.

This time the bullet hit her lower stomach and she knew she would bleed out next to her dead husband. When her body fell back and the blood seeping out of her wounds started to mix with the crimson liquid that had poured out of Frank, all she could think about was the Peach. She would be reunited with the love of her life but Peach didn't have a chance to even arrive in this world. The tears that slipped out of her eyes were not because she was scared to die, they were because she was mourning the child that would never be born.

Her mind was fuzzy and she felt like she was only processing every tenth picture in front of her eyes. She was sure that this was what dying felt like. Confusion, pain, blurriness and then a sense of calm.

People were shouting. A shot rang out and the intruder collapsed to the floor. A blonde woman in a police uniform appeared in front of her. There were more sirens and then her body was being carried down the stairs and placed onto a gurney. People were talking to her but they were miles away.

Eventually she made it into an ambulance and when her eyes finally closed, all she could hear was “All I want for Christmas is you”.

Her last thought before darkness consumed her was:

It was the first Christmas of many that she would spend alone.

All alone.

YOU DRIVE ME CRAZY

NOW
March 2022

Oliver's finger gently circled around the ugly scar on Marta's lower belly, making her remember the bullet that had entered her body more than three years ago. She huffed and turned her body away from him. The blond Agent was taken aback, turning on his side and wrapping one arm around Marta's waist while he carefully placed a tender kiss between her shoulder blades.

The second gunshot wound was right in front of his eyes, but Marta had always been vulnerable with both of them whenever she stripped out of her clothes.

"What's wrong?" he murmured against her warm skin.

"Nothing."

"Marta." His voice was sterner now, warning.

He knew she was lying. Although they'd only been dating for a few months, they had been friends for years.

"I don't like the scars." She mumbled in her pillow, but Oliver knew it wasn't the full truth.

"I think you're beautiful no matter how many scars you have on your body." He emphasized his statement with a few kisses along her shoulders and neck.

"You have to say that because you want to have sex with me." Marta sighed, not able to accept the compliment Oliver was giving her.

She felt herself being pulled into his arms as his lips continued their gentle assault on her neck.

"It's not about the sex, Marta. Well, the sex is good, but that's not the point. I like you. A lot. I told you I'd ask you out over and over again until you say yes to a date with me. An official date, not a date as friends."

She wanted to be angry at him for bringing up that topic again. Half a year ago Marta had made herself very clear. *Very clear*, that she didn't want to have a romantic relationship with him, but it was Oliver and his charming smile, his ability to make her feel loved, to make her smile and laugh that drew her to him over and over again. It had ended with them having sex for the first time, drunk, on New Year's Eve. Oliver, as the hopelessly romantic man that he was, saw this as his new chance to finally turn the gears towards a relationship, but Marta insisted on being friends with benefits.

"Say something." He whispered nervously at her neck, leaving featherlight touches with his lips along her cervical spine.

"What do you want me to say?" She sighed.

"Anything. Just don't leave me hanging."

"If I remember last night correctly, I didn't leave you hanging for a single second, Oliver."

A loud laughter could be heard behind her, hurting her ears by the intensity and volume. Oliver hadn't expected this response at all.

"Touché." He said between shallow breaths.

But instead of just accepting his defeat he whispered:

"Go on a date with me, Marta Gómez. Please."

Marta sighed deeply, looking for the right answer without hurting him too much. When she opened her mouth to respond the word "Okay" left her mouth, surprising not only Oliver but also herself. She didn't want to say that, she didn't want to agree to a date with him. Why the hell did her body do that? Why did her mouth betray her like that?

Oliver stiffened behind her, unsure if it was only a joke or if she really meant it. Did she mean it? She wasn't sure herself.

"You serious?" he asked, his voice dripping with confusion and fear of getting rejected again.

"Yeah. No. I mean. I don't know."

Oliver tried to turn her body around so that he was able to face her but she refused and stayed in her position so he pushed himself off the mattress and climbed over her so that he was lying in front of her. His dorky behavior made her laugh and the way he looked at her right now were bandaids on the cracks that still decorated her heart. This man was driving her crazy.

"What does that mean? Are you going on a date with me or not?"

She had never seen him look at her with so much hope behind his blue-green eyes. He'd asked her for a date so many times, but every time he knew she would decline. Her reaction shocked him, just as much as it shocked her.

"Yeah. I think so. I'm coming on a date with you." She smiled at him, seeing his eyes widen. First in surprise, then happiness.

"Really?"

"If you ask me one more time, I'll say no."

Oliver tried to stifle some high-pitched noises while he slammed his palm onto the mattress in excitement. Marta gasped in shock and one of her eyebrows rose until it was almost lost in her hairline. Why was he reacting like this?

He looked into her bemused face and a wide grin spread over his own face before he jumped out of the bed.

"What the..." Marta started, but got distracted by the perfect arrow that Oliver's upper body was shaped into.

The constant working out from the age of 16 was really showing off in his toned abs, the popping pelvic bones and the muscular chest. And his biceps... Marta could get lost in watching them tense every time Oliver picked something up.

Her train of thought was interrupted the moment Oliver started to dance around the bed. His hands balled into fists, his arms swinging wildly around his upper body while he moved his hips to a music that only he could hear.

It looked ridiculous and adorable at the same time.

"We're gonna have a date. We're gonna have a date," he hummed, punctuating his words with more hip movements.

That man knew exactly how to move his hips but that wasn't news for Marta. Sex with him had shown that to her pretty quickly.

"You're crazy," she mumbled between laughs, her eyes following Oliver's every move.

Marta wouldn't describe his dancing as elegant or even following any kind of rhythm, but she couldn't stop giving him heart-eyes. He looked way too cute in his excitement and happiness.

"Marta Gómez is gonna go on a date with meeeeee," Oliver sang while winking at the woman still lying in the bed.

"Shut up and come here now."

"Yes, ma'am."

Oliver stopped dancing and placed himself at the end of the bed before jumping head first into it.

"Shit!" Marta exclaimed, but thankfully she managed to pull her one leg away in time before Oliver landed with his stomach on the mattress.

He was giggling like a teenager, rolling on his side to face Marta with a broad grin and sparkles in his eyes.

"Stop behaving like a teenager, Oliver!"

"Okay, sorry," he laughed, leaning in and giving her a kiss on her lips, but the moment his lips touched hers he pulled back and looked at her.

They'd kissed each other before but always in the heat of the moment while having sex, not outside of it.

"Oh gosh." He only whispered, let himself fall back on his back and covered his eyes with his hands in embarrassment.

"I'm such an idiot." He mumbled again and again, whining in between the words and trying to melt into the mattress so that Marta wouldn't find him anymore.

She watched him for a while before having mercy with him and scooted closer to him to place a kiss on his forearm. She couldn't reach anything else.

"It's okay." She whispered in between more kisses.

"It's not. I kissed you without your consent. I *am* an idiot." He was still mumbling into his hands, making it hard to understand him.

"Oliver." Marta now said with a tone that made him flinch.

He removed his hands from his face, turned his head towards Marta and looked at her in expectation of the rant that he knew was probably coming. But instead of saying something the Deputy Director crawled on top of him so that her body was covering most of his. Then she slowly leaned her head down and connected her lips with his. In an instant another crack in her heart grew back together, giving her hope that one day it would be healed completely. All because of the man laying underneath her. Oliver slung his arms around Marta's body, crossing his arms on the small of her back, and returned her kiss passionately.

After a while they let each other go from the kiss, looking into each other's eyes for another moment.

"Now tell me. What the hell happened in the last thirty minutes?" he asked, still a little confused. When did Marta's answer change from only friends with benefits to agreeing to a date with him and then even deliberately kissing him?

"I have no idea." Marta chuckled, before wiggling her body downwards a little so that she could place her head on his chest. Oliver rubbed different shapes like circles and rectangles with his fingernails on the top of her back, still trying to get his head around the change in their relationship. It was unexpected but more than welcome.

"You make me happy for the first time since Frank died. Like really, really happy. When I'm lying here with you I can forget the sadness inside my heart because you make me feel loved. Maybe I wasn't willing to accept that but the better I felt, the more I could ignore it. So you deserve this date. You fought hard for it, soldier."

Instead of answering her, Oliver placed ten kisses on the top of Marta's head, making her giggle like a teenager.

"It was worth the fight," he whispered, before trying to pull her even closer, which wasn't physically possible but Marta appreciated the gesture.

"What do you have in mind? For the date?" She asked into his chest, enjoying the tender caresses he was still making across her back.

"I'd love to go out and watch a movie with you."

"I like watching movies but I'd prefer to do that here."

Marta wasn't comfortable with leaving headquarters, too scared that the mafia were still after her, although it was quite unlikely after all this time.

"But if we go out we won't have to watch our backs the entire time," Oliver sighed.

"Oh, you're right."

It was the first time Marta actually thought about the fact that she was practically dating someone she was responsible for. They'd been friends for years so it never was a problem, but she was his boss. She was making decisions with and for him and she was pretty sure the CIA wouldn't allow them to pursue a relationship. There would be too many conflicts of interest. Holy shit, what did she maneuver herself into?

"You're spiraling," Oliver commented, trying to get her back to a happier place.

"Sorry. I was just thinking that we might not be allowed to date, because of the hierarchy and all the stuff that comes with that. What if I make a wrong decision in my job only because I fell in love with you and am scared to lose you? What if other people get hurt or even worse, just because I made that wrong decision?" Her voice filled with more panic as she went through all the what-ifs in her head.

"I don't care," Oliver said with a loving voice.

"But..."

"No buts. We just decided on ONE date. One date, Marta. Please stop thinking about everything that comes after that." He sighed loudly. Had he thought about the hierarchy aspect before? Sure, but he really didn't care. He always listened to his heart and gut and both had been telling him for months that this woman was someone he could imagine spending his entire life with. She came into his life broken, sad and traumatized but over the last two years he saw her heal piece by piece. It wasn't that she was his fixer upper project, he'd gotten to know glimpses of her true self right after she moved into the headquarters, and he'd realized early on that this woman deserved happiness.

"Okay. One date, but we can't tell anybody."

"Sure. We got this, Marta," he said and placed another kiss on her lips.

She couldn't resist his charm and his infectious positivity. Being around Oliver seemed to make all the depressive and sad vibes of the world go away. He was like the first sunny days in spring that kicked people's hearts and souls back to life after a long winter.

"We got this," she repeated while a smile danced along her lips.

This man could cost her independence, maybe even her job, but he was driving her crazy and she was willing to re-discover a side of herself that she'd long kept buried away.

I' M HERE FOR YOU

THEN
March 2019

"Agent Gómez, this is your room. We already have some furniture in it, but you can buy whatever you want. Feel free to replace everything." Director Burns said to Marta while they were standing awkwardly in the hallway.

He had extended his right hand out to her, expecting a shake, but as Marta's right shoulder was still weak after being buried in a sling for a long time she extended her left one and gave the Director the weirdest handshake ever. The man shot her a pitiful look before he nodded and stepped along the hallway to the elevators.

Marta placed her ID Card on the lock panel, saw the light turn green, and opened it with her left hand. Her whole body was still trembling slightly, her legs still weak even after weeks of hard physical therapy but lying in a coma for two weeks did that to people. The doctors and her physical therapist were more than happy about her recovery, telling her over and over again that she was exceptional for being able to walk so early in the recovery process. She didn't feel like that. All she wanted to do was get back on her feet as soon as possible so that she could run away from her past. Run away from everything that happened and start a new life somewhere. Where no one was in danger anymore just because they were related to her in some way.

The room she was standing in was bleak, the walls painted a sterile white, the furniture radiating the same vibe, like this had never been a home to someone. This was only a temporary station for most of the Agents so there was no need to make this room homey and cozy. No personal pictures, no plants. The room was as sterile as possible so that it was easy to clean.

Marta had never felt more depressed since the day her husband died. Standing in this depressingly clean room showed her, with all its brutality, that her old life and her happiness had died with Frank and the Peach last Christmas Eve.

Before she could dive deeper into the storm of intrusive thoughts inside her mind a loud knock came from the door. She had left it ajar so there was no particular reason for someone to knock. Did Director Burns forget something?

"Come in," she said quieter than she wanted to, but whoever was standing in the hallway had heard it because she suddenly saw the light from the hallway shine into the room.

It wasn't dark, but she hadn't turned on the lights and the cloudy day outside didn't really do much to lighten the room through the window.

"Hi."

She heard a male voice from behind her, which didn't belong to Director Burns.

She slowly turned on her heels to see who was standing in her room and her eyes met a tall 6'2" / 1.90m man with short blond hair, broad shoulders, and a wide grin on his face. Marta quickly let her eyes wander over his body and observed his defined biceps, the muscular thighs that were popping out of the workout shorts he wore, as well as the messiness of his hair, which reminded her so much of Frank's when he came out of the shower.

"Hi," she responded, unsure how to properly react.

"Oliver McGreen, I've seen you with Burns and came to introduce myself and check to see if you need anything."

He extended his right hand towards her as the traditional way to introduce himself.

Marta was annoyed by all the handshakes she had to decline because of her shoulder but this time she really didn't want to get another pitiful look so she gathered all her strength, clenched her teeth to ignore the agonizing pain in the still sore and rusty joint, and managed to reach out her hand to grab his.

"Marta Gómez," she hissed and her weird reaction made Oliver furrow his face a little but he tried to ignore it and started to happily shake her hand. The moment a loud whine left Marta's mouth, he let go of her hand and looked at her, shocked.

"Sorry," she mumbled, unconsciously holding her arm in the recovery position it had been used in with the sling over the past three months.

"Sorry," Oliver copied her, not sure what had just happened.

This was definitely his strangest encounter of the week, and he'd been dealing with the weird behavior of his best friend Nate for almost eight years now.

"I'm hurt. My shoulder. Thought I could just ignore it but turns out it still hurts like shit," she tried to explain when she saw the weird grimace on Oliver's face.

This man was definitely not good at hiding his emotions. His face and eyes gave him away. He was uncomfortable about the whole situation.

"Oh, I'm sorry to hear that. You could've told me, then I would've used my other hand."

He smiled at her, waving his left hand in the air. His smile was infectious, although Marta didn't feel like smiling.

"Didn't want to look broken," she mumbled, sadness present in her honey-colored eyes.

Oliver cleared his throat, extended his left hand, and said:

"Hi. I'm Oliver McGreen. Nice to meet you."

Marta tilted her head a little in surprise but extended her left hand and shook his. It felt weird, as she was right-handed, but they both tried to make it as comfortable as possible.

"Marta Gómez, drug trafficking task force," she introduced herself again, still with a shy smile on her lips.

"It's nice to meet you, Marta," and with that being said, he let go of her hand and walked around the still depressing and mostly dark room.

The clouds outside had darkened within seconds and the heavens opened up. The rain drummed on the window now, catching Marta by surprise as she was so focused on Oliver that she hadn't noticed the change in weather.

"It's not the prettiest but it does its job for the time being. Director Burns normally doesn't mention it but, depending on how long you stay here, it's okay to bring some decorations. Making it more like a home than a sterile med-bay room."

His comparison with a hospital made sense and she wondered why she hadn't thought about it before. She'd spent most of her time in hospital rooms since December but in the rehab hospital the rooms were colorful, decorated, and full of normal stuff. Only the hospital beds had reminded her that she was not in a hotel.

"Yeah, I realized that. It needs some color and definitely some plants. Maybe I can get some when I'm feeling better." Her voice echoed in the room.

She saw Oliver nod as he looked into the attached bathroom and the walk-in closet with curiosity all over his face.

"It's the same size as my room but the bathroom is more modern. You've got a walk-in shower, mine's an older one. Feels like I should ask Burns for a renovation. They haven't done anything in eight years. It's about damn time," he said towards Marta with the grin still on his face.

Oliver was probably the friendliest human she had ever met.

"You should. No walk-in shower. How dare they."

Oliver halted in his movement and looked at Marta before he burst into laughter. The heaviness and insecurity of their first encounter was blown away by his beautiful laughter and Marta's heart burned when she saw him close his eyes and lean forward. The joke had caught him off guard and although it wasn't actually that funny, the whole situation made him laugh.

"You should enjoy this shower as long as you can," he said between shallow breaths.

"Oh, I will. I didn't even have a real shower at home. We had one of those bathtubs that could also be used as a shower. It fit into our house because it was more of a vintage style, but I missed a real shower every damn time," she sighed.

"So it's the perfect time to enjoy the luxury of this amazing walk-in shower. It might even have one of those fancy rainfall showerheads."

He sounded like a real estate agent who was trying to sell this apartment to her.

"Sounds amazing, although it takes double the time to get the shampoo out of my hair with those shower heads. They just don't have the same power as the others."

"Yeah, well, I don't have that problem. The advantage of being a short-haired man," he laughed, rubbing his hand through the blond hair that looked even messier afterwards.

"How long do you plan to stay?" He added.

"Ehm..." Marta avoided his gaze, suddenly being reminded that this was not a temporary home.

"Oh, don't worry. A lot of Agents don't know straight away. The operations are exhausting and Director Burns usually lets them rest before talking about details."

He tried to assure her, realizing that her shoulders had dropped and she looked like she was feeling uncomfortable.

"No, that's not it. I... This is more of a permanent stay," she whispered, barely hearable.

"Oh," Oliver responded, unsure what would be appropriate to say now.

"Sorry to hear that," he added, knowing that only people with immense trauma would live in the headquarters forever.

She'd already told him that she was hurt, making Oliver wonder what had happened to her that made her have to move in permanently, but of course he wouldn't ask. That wouldn't be polite and his parents raised him to be as gentlemanly as possible.

"Yeah."

She had her face turned away from him, probably hiding some tears.

"So..." Oliver started again with a happier tone "... let's make this place your new home then. Do you have a new color in mind?"

Marta turned towards him, the stains of her tears still visible on her face but she'd managed to stop crying. It was a short outburst of sadness but she didn't want him to feel uncomfortable around her and a crying woman was never very comfortable.

"I was thinking about a berry shade behind the bed. Maybe raspberry? That could look amazing with some green plants and gold decor."

Her mind had shifted to an image of the room in its future state and what she wanted to change so that she felt comfortable. She wouldn't go so far as to call it home soon but it would be the first step in the right direction.

"Raspberry sounds amazing. The whole room or only one wall?"

"Only one wall. The whole room would be too much, wouldn't it?" Marta laughed a little, her sadness blowing away when she distracted herself with her renovation plans.

"It could be too much. If you want to, I can drive you around and we can buy some paint, plants, and decorations? Helping you settle." He smiled at her.

Marta was thankful for his offer as she wouldn't be able to do this herself.

"That'd be nice, thank you. I'm still recovering from being shot and I can't carry anything with this shoulder. A helping hand sounds amazing."

"Tomorrow?" he asked, surprising her once more.

"Yeah. Yeah, why not? Let's make this room comfy."

Marta's night was uncomfortable. Sleep didn't come to her easily and when the physical exhaustion let her fall asleep dreams of Frank screaming at her to save him haunted her and forced her back to consciousness. Everything smelled weird and everything felt weird. Every time she woke in the middle of the night she was confused, not knowing where she was or how she had come here. Thankfully Director Burns had already shown her where the community kitchen was, so she shuffled along the hallway in a desperate attempt to get a coffee into her tired system. She hadn't slept that badly in weeks. The rehab hospital had felt like home for her after a while, mostly because the pills she got every evening blocked the nightmares and made her sleep carefree like a baby. She missed those pills.

With one button she kicked the coffee machine back to life and watched the brown liquid fill the mug underneath it. She licked her lips in anticipation, eager to swallow it down and feel her body come back to life. At least, as alive as it could get after a sleepless night, three months of rehab, and a still-more-than-fragile body.

"Good morning."

Oliver's voice came from behind her. She quickly spun around, a little too fast for her brain, and immediately saw stars. Thankfully Oliver had seen her eyes roll back, sprinted towards her, and caught her before her legs could give up.

"Gotcha," he mumbled and steadied her on her hips.

"Sorry. It's still hard for me to remember how broken I actually am," she sighed.

The coffee machine had finished its job and, with a shaking hand, Marta grabbed the mug and placed it on the kitchen counter next to it.

"You want one, too?" She asked Oliver, who had stepped back but still watched her with a concerned frown on his face.

"No, thank you. I'm more of a tea kind of person."

"No coffee? That's a big meh."

"Meh?" Oliver asked, confused.

"Yeah, meh. My roomie in the rehab hospital was in her early twenties and she taught me some phrases and words that you say nowadays. One of them is *meh* and it should express that you don't really like something."

"Meh," Oliver repeated a few times, trying to evaluate if he'd like it enough to include it in his thesaurus or not.

Marta laughed a little while watching the man in front of her mumble the new word over and over again. He looked pretty cute. Cute? Wait a minute. She hadn't used that word for a man in months. The last one she called cute was Frank. Speaking of Frank...

"I thought we could maybe make a stop at my old house, and I could get some of my stuff from there. They didn't let me go when I was discharged from rehab," she suggested, her voice low and filled with insecurity, something Oliver didn't understand. As if Marta's whole life was a loud sigh.

"Are you allowed to go there?" Oliver carefully asked.

"I... I don't know," Marta answered honestly.

Oliver was right. What if some of the mafioso were waiting for her, trying to get revenge for their murdered and arrested colleagues.

"You'd better ask Director Burns for his opinion. If he agrees we can go there as a last stop before returning home."

Home.

Oliver had called the headquarters home but for her, home was where she wanted to stop and grab her stuff. The house with the wonderful white door and the bathtub shower. Filled with her and Frank's laughter and waiting for a tiny little human to turn their lives upside down. They'd just started to prepare the nursery. Way too early, but they were so excited. But that house - her home - would never be filled with laughter again. Would never be filled with the screams of a baby. That house was silent now. And would be forever.

"Marta?" he asked concerned, seeing that the brunette woman had drifted off again.

She did that a lot in their conversations. This also wasn't new to him, having dealt with Nate and his demons for years now. He wondered what had happened to her that she was so easily distracted.

"Yeah? Sorry. Sounds good."

Marta shook her head a little, forcing herself to stay in the reality she was currently in. CIA headquarters, her new home.

"Let me know when you're ready. I have a great place to go for breakfast. Director Burns should already be in his office. He's an early bird," he said before kicking the coffee machine back to life.

"Sure."

Marta was about to leave the kitchen to see Director Burns and ask if she was allowed to go home when she turned around once more.

"Thought you weren't a coffee kind of guy?"

"It's for Butch, I mean Nate. Nate Sheppard, a colleague and friend. People call him Butch. He lives here too. We're in the terrorism task force together. Tall, grumpy-looking guy. You'll meet him soon."

"And he can't get his coffee on his own?"

"Nah. The Oliver McGreen breakfast service is an experience everybody needs to have once in a lifetime and Butch Sheppard will get it today."

Oliver winked at Marta, and she felt herself laugh. Honestly laugh. For the first time in a long time.

Thankfully, Director Burns gave his okay to visit her house and get some of her personal possessions but he reminded her that too many visits could alarm the mafia if they were still observing her house. Officially, the CIA had declared her dead, making sure that the mafiosos were left in the dark about whether she survived the major injuries she suffered from. It had been tough, the doctors told her parents to say goodbye to her more than once, but she fought her way back to life every time. She wondered a lot about what for. Was her life worth living now without Frank? Without the Peach?

What was left that she was looking forward to? What was left to make her happy and smile, or forget the tragedy of her life?

While sitting in an armored SUV that the CIA gave them to leave the headquarters, she turned her head to the side and watched the man who steered the car through the traffic of Washington, D.C.

She couldn't deny that Oliver made her smile and she'd only known him for a few hours. He'd offered his help, he'd tried to lighten her mood while still keeping his polite distance. Not asking for any details, not pushing any agenda.

Oliver turned his head and gave her a side-eye, smiling a little before he concentrated on the street in front of him again. Silence lingered between them but it wasn't uncomfortable. Marta was concentrating on her breathing, making sure she wouldn't have a mental breakdown as soon as the car was parked on the driveway of her and Frank's house. She'd talked to her therapist multiple times about returning and every time she'd said she wasn't ready yet. Marta had no clue what had changed but right now she felt strong enough to face the house. The white door with the little window in it. The empty hallways and the silent rooms.

She was ready.

She wanted to be strong and this was her first step toward accepting her new life and moving on. At least that's what she was repeating over and over again in her mind in a desperate attempt to keep the panic attack at arm's length.

"It's the third house on the left," she whispered towards Oliver, who only nodded in response and slowly drove the large black car onto the empty driveway.

Marta closed her eyes and took a deep breath but before she was able to open her door she heard Oliver open the one on the driver's side.

She quickly opened her eyes and looked at him with furrowed eyebrows.

"Wait, where are you going?" she asked.

"Helping you get the stuff out of the house and into the car. Want to make sure you're okay, too," he mumbled, but she saw in his features that he regretted not having asked her before.

"That's really kind of you but I have to do this alone. It's... it's something mental. My therapist said I need to face the demons of my past in order to heal. So I need to go in there alone."

"Okay. Understood. But... Gimme your phone."

Marta wasn't sure what he was up to, but she grabbed the new phone out of her pocket that Director Burns had given her. Keeping the old one would have been too dangerous.

She also wondered what the neighbors would think when they randomly looked out of their windows and saw a "dead" woman walking along the front porch of the house. Maybe they'd think they saw a ghost. She'd scare her neighbors to death.

Oliver typed something into Marta's phone and started a call between the two phones.

"You don't have to talk to me, but please put the phone in your pocket and keep the call open so I know if something happens to you and come to save you. Is that okay with you?" He looked at her narrowed eyes, not sure if she was okay with his suggestion or not.

"Okay," Marta nodded, appreciating that this Agent cared about her. He was a really good man. She felt it in her heart.

Seeing all the candles, handwritten letters, pictures, and flowers on the front porch of her house made tears well in her eyes. A lot of the pictures showed her, Frank, and friends. Smiling and laughing, beers in their hands, at parties or barbecues. All those happy memories had now turned into painful ones. Painful to remember her old life. The life before last Christmas.

She grabbed the key that Director Burns had given her and opened the door. The CIA had changed the locks after the tragedy. The mafioso had entered the house without breaking anything, so they must have had a key. To prevent them from returning, the CIA had changed the locks as soon as Marta was in the hospital and the clean-up team was done restoring the house as much as possible. After securing all the evidence first of course.

The hallway looked exactly how she remembered it, just a little dustier. The gray particles were laying heavy on all the furniture Marta had chosen for the house. Her eyes fixed on the sideboard next to the door, remembering how she had entered the house a few months ago, and had headed towards the hidden pistol in it. With a shake of her head, she went into the living room next, collected some of the dusty decorations like vases, candles, and other stuff and placed all of them on the wooden coffee table. They had their favorite wedding picture hanging as a canvas over their couch making sure they never forgot how happy they were on that day.

Seeing the picture again made Marta smile. They were really happy and she would have those memories forever. While still staring at the large picture of her and her really handsome husband she realized that she wanted to take the photo albums with her. It was one of Frank's weird ideas, to make a photo album after every holiday and, obviously, they had one of their wedding too. He'd said they could look at the albums again, remembering their past vacations and the amazing times they spent together. He'd preferred that over thousands of pictures on his phone but, to be honest, they hadn't looked at the albums after their vacations.

The vacation albums were in the living room but she remembered that Frank had stored the wedding one in their bedroom because they actually looked at this one quite regularly. Sometimes before they went to bed, cuddling under one big blanket, they indulged themselves in the memories of their first day as Mr. and Mrs. Gómez.

Marta quickly paced up the stairs, skipping almost every second step. With her lips pressed in a thin line, her shoulders suddenly slumped and a pressure bloomed in her chest, Marta placed her left hand on the handle of the bedroom door.

As slowly as possible she opened the door to her bedroom, trying really hard to ignore the screaming and agonizing memories that threatened to come to the surface again. She didn't want to think about this. The moment she'd found Frank had haunted her dreams for so long now. Marta was proud of herself because she was able to open the door and enter the room that had once been her favorite place.

Until it became her worst nightmare.

But here she was, standing in the doorway of her own bedroom, letting her gaze wander around the room. She realized that the clean-up team hadn't actually cleaned up. The walk-in closet was still a mess, with different clothes lying on the floor, a few of them belonged to her, a few that were Frank's. She could see some of his favorite flannel shirts. She grabbed three of them and threw them on the bed. She was taking them with her. To have something from Frank in her new life. As a reminder. So she would never forget. They were all clean so none of the shirts would smell like him but at least she had them with her.

It took Marta a tremendous effort to finally let her eyes drop to the place where Frank had been lying, where she collapsed on the floor right next to him. Of course the blood was gone and the herringbone parquet was not stained with crimson anymore.

She let out the breath she was holding, feeling relief flood her body in an instant.

Until she saw a shimmer of red. A shimmer she couldn't ignore.

Marta knelt down to look at what had caught her eye. It was the gaps between the beige-colored parquet. Although the clean-up team had done their best to get rid of the blood particles, some of them had gathered in between the gaps in the wood, staining it a slightly pinkish color. Nothing that would make it necessary to change the entire flooring but enough to catapult Marta back to the nightmare of last Christmas.

"No. No. No. No."

She was panting, every blink of her eyelashes bringing back the picture of dead Frank lying in front of her knees.

The blood, his lifeless gray eyes, the shocked look on his face, and then she felt the pain again. The searing, hot, burning pain of the gunshots that entered her body. Pushing through tissue, muscle, and bone. Leaving a crust of ashes and stains of blood. All of it was happening again.

Right here. Right now.

Marta began to cry again. Her tears slipped down her face and onto her shirt. She was sobbing, her body shaking uncontrollably. There it was. The mental breakdown.

Suddenly, a large hand appeared on the upper part of her back making her shrink back while she tried to defend herself. She tried to kick and beat the intruder, scared that the mafia found her again and were trying to finally get their revenge.

"Hey. Shh. Shhhhh. It's me. It's Oliver."

She heard a voice but her panicking brain wasn't able to process the words.

With all the strength her still weak body contained, she boxed out at the person close to her. She felt her fist hit him multiple times but he didn't even try to get away. He knelt right next to her, enduring her punches, until her body was too exhausted to defend herself anymore. The adrenaline faded and with it Marta's ability to land any hits. Oliver was surprised at how much her punches had hurt him and he was sure he'd have some bruises. It was the first glimpse she'd given him of her true strength, of the bad-ass Agent she'd been before whatever happened in this house. He didn't know and he didn't ask. Not her, not Director Burns. She'd tell him if and when she was ready, and if not, then that was okay for him too. He'd already been through all that with his best friend Butch. He had experience with someone reliving their horrors all over again.

When Marta finally stilled he carefully wrapped his arms around her and pulled her in for a hug. Maybe he was crossing a line here but he had a huge urge to help this poor woman. To hold her and make her feel better. To be there for her.

Marta crawled on his lap, straddling him, while he pressed her close against his chest. Was this strange for two colleagues who only knew each other for a day? Absolutely.

But it felt right at that moment.

"Shh. It's okay. I'm here. You are safe."

CHRISTMAS SWEATER

THEN

December 24th, 2019

The colors of their wedding picture had already faded, way more than they should have after only two years, but after Frank's death Marta had had the picture between her fingers more often than usual, diving deep into the memories of the happiest day of her life. Seeing their first dance in front of her eyes, both of them not knowing any kind of dancing, just swaying to the music while laughing so much that their abs hurt afterwards. Frank had always made her laugh.

That night she had dreamed about waking up in their old house and when she had turned her head around Frank was snoring beside her. Marta had always been annoyed by his very loud snoring, which stole her sleep way too often, but in her dream all she could do was smile and cry when she heard his snores. She'd missed him so much. Marta had cuddled by his side, carefully slipping underneath his arm, and placed her head on his chest. His steady heartbeat and the rumbling snores had made her feel happier than she had in the last 365 days.

When she really woke up in the CIA headquarters, alone, her heart broke all over again. Exactly a year had gone by since the day the intruder killed Frank and it felt like only yesterday that she found him in their bedroom. This morning the first thing she did was grab her purse and get the folded wedding picture out of it. She'd been carrying it with her ever since his death. They hadn't been the classic 'I carry a picture of my partner in my purse' couple before, but grabbing her favorite picture and placing it in her purse was the first thing she did when she woke from the coma. A nurse from the rehab hospital had negotiated with the CIA that they bring Marta a few personal items while she was recovering from her severe injuries. The nurse had been very convincing in saying that Marta needed something to hold while she went through all the different stages of grief.

Marta saw a tear fall on the picture in her hands before the liquid exploded into tinier drops. Before she could dive deeper into the carousel of her mind, she heard a knock from the door.

"Come in!" She shouted, trying to dry her eyes to not look like a zombie but she was sure she'd failed miserably. She hastened to her door and opened it.

With a big smile on his face Oliver held a self-made Christmas cookie up to Marta's face. It was in the shape of a Christmas tree and someone had tried to put some green icing with sprinkles on top of it. You could see that said-person was not used to working with icing as it looked like it had been flowing off the cookie, taking most of the decorations with it.

"Cookie for breakfast?" He asked while tilting his upper body behind the cookie so that Marta could see his face.

She wasn't in the mood for anything to do with Christmas but Oliver's wide smile and the absolute happiness in his eyes made her lips twitch until she was smiling too.

"That's what you call a healthy breakfast, Agent?" She chuckled a little.

"We can be healthy the other 362 days of the year but not the three days of Christmas!" Oliver responded, still holding the cookie towards Marta.

She sighed and grabbed the cookie out of his hands. Oliver looked at her with expectation in his eyes and Marta knew he wouldn't go away before she at least gave it a try. As carefully as possible she took a small bite of the cookie and the moment the dough melted on her tongue she couldn't help but moan a little.

"Wow it's amazing," she commented before taking a bigger bite.

"It's my mom's recipe. Christmas cookies on Christmas Eve are a McGreen tradition but they're almost all gone. I wanted to bake another batch in an hour. You wanna help?"

"Actually…" Marta started and avoided Oliver's gaze.

The tears gathered around her lashes again but she didn't want him to see her crying. He'd ignored the zombie look pretty well so far.

"… I'm not in the Christmas mood this year, but thanks for asking."

She gave him a weak smile, trying as hard as possible to keep it together and push away the intrusive thoughts of her dead husband and the child that was never born.

"Don't be a Grinch!" Oliver pouted at her.

This 30-something-year-old man looked so much like a child at that moment that Marta laughed out loud. She was amazed at how he was able to make her laugh so easily. Oliver took this as a silent compliment and started to laugh as well.

"I am not. Just not in the mood," she insisted.

"Okkkaaaaaaaaayyyy," Oliver sighed loudly before adding, "Then I'll have to ask the Grinch himself to bake some cookies with me. I need a helping hand."

Marta only raised an eyebrow at him, not understanding who he meant.

"I mean Butch. He wasn't in the mood for Christmas for years. Gotta force him today though," Oliver chuckled.

"Oh yeah. He's really… special."

Marta tried to be polite. She only knew Nate "Butch" Sheppard in passing, when she and her colleague Jakob spent their lunch breaks with him and Oliver. The brunette man and her hadn't really spoken a lot, well, the man hadn't spoken at all. Even after all these years she couldn't even think of how his voice sounded.

"He's been through a lot. You'd like him if you knew him," Oliver said, something flickering in his eyes that Marta didn't understand.

"Yeah, maybe."

Oliver cleared his throat, clearly uncomfortable that the conversation had switched over to his best friend.

"But you have to cook dinner with me tonight, okay? It's Christmas Eve. We gotta have a big feast!" He was smiling again.

"I..." Marta started but didn't have a chance to continue when Oliver placed his hand on her upper arm.

"There's no way you can get out of this. Also, you just got promoted and we didn't even celebrate that! I'll pick you up at 6 and then we make dinner together."

"Okay," Marta sighed, rolling her eyes.

She really wasn't in the mood for any kind of Christmas activity but she was sure she wouldn't be able to convince Oliver to leave her alone.

"Great. See you later, and you know where to find me if you're craving cookies."

He winked at her and walked along the hallway with a spring in his step.

Marta shook her head but found herself still smiling. Oliver had a positive influence on her. She slotted the wedding picture back in her purse and grabbed her laptop to do some work. Two days ago Director Burns had called her into his office and she had almost shit her pants but, instead of getting screamed at or fired, the Director told her about her promotion.

She hadn't expected to really get the position as the role had been filled by men for centuries.

Marta Gómez became the first female Deputy Director of Operations two days ago. She had told Director Burns to keep it small, no big ceremony or stuff like that, so it was super low-key.

With the new job came more work and more responsibilities. She'd been the team leader of the drug trafficking task force ever since she moved to headquarters. It was more than clear that, after what happened, she wouldn't be going back into the field. Jakob had become the operational leader of the team with Marta in the background organizing staffing, transport and things like that as well as supporting them while being on operations.

Now she was not only responsible for the drug trafficking task force but for four more. One of them was the terrorism task force in which Oliver and Butch were working. She'd done as much research as possible ever since her promotion to be able to answer questions from all the different task forces but it wasn't easy as they mostly asked questions to topics she didn't know much about other than the CIA basics. So, even when it was Christmas Eve, Marta Gómez spent the entire day on her desk making notes about the different operations and specialisms of each team.

Around 5 p.m. she realized with a shock that she was close to being late so she jumped into the shower and changed into some jeans and a light gray basic t-shirt. Oliver had said he'd pick her up at six but her stomach was grumbling so she headed to the kitchen early. He'd find her. It was in the same hallway.

With every step closer to the community kitchen, music became louder and louder. Marta was almost standing in the doorway when she realized that the song "Rockin' Around The Christmas Tree" was playing. While rolling her eyes again she stepped into the kitchen and was greeted by a dancing blond man.

Oliver was currently decorating the dinner table, his back towards Marta, while he was dancing passionately to the song. He wore black jeans, a dark blue sweater and a weird headpiece with reindeer antlers on it. She saw him sway his hips to the rhythm of the song in a way that made her think he'd be experienced moving them in other ways.

When he turned around to head to the kitchen again his eyes met Marta's and he visibly jumped in the air while screaming "AH!"

Marta couldn't stop herself from laughing, the situation in front of her was too funny. The shock on Oliver's face, the too high-pitched scream and the little jump. It was hilarious.

"Sorry, I didn't see you!"

Now that he was turned around towards her she could finally see that his sweater showed a gray tabby cat wearing sunglasses with the words "Meowy Christmas" underneath.

To be honest, it looked pretty cute.

"Nice sweater," Marta snickered, pointing her finger at the cat in the middle of Oliver's chest.

"Glad you're saying that because I have one for you too!"

He ran towards the couches to grab a green and red sweater from them before proudly turning it around so that Marta could see what was on it. The sweater showed a llama wearing a Christmas beanie and scarf, and above she could read “No probllama”.

“I know it’s not really Spanish but it was the closest I could find,” he explained, a little insecure, unsure if the sweater was appropriate or not.

“I love it. Thank you.” Marta smiled honestly at him.

She’d told him about her mom being from Spain, immigrating to the States because she couldn’t find a job as a Spanish teacher at home. A High School near Washington was looking for someone and they hired her mom so even though Marta was born in the U.S. her mom always spoke Spanish to her, maintaining their culture as much as possible.

With a quick motion she pulled the sweater over her upper body and looked at Oliver with a smile still on her lips.

“How do I look?”

“Beautiful. As always,” Oliver whispered, regretting his words immediately, and Marta could see his cheeks turn pink like a radish.

“Thanks. You look good too, especially the antlers on your head. Gives you a very manly look,” she laughed.

Oliver's eyes widened before he joined her laughter.

"Thanks for making me laugh. I needed that today," she added, a sad glimmer behind her eyes that Oliver didn't understand.

He didn't want to push the topic so he simply nodded and placed his hand on her upper arm, slightly brushing over the fabric of the sweater. Marta looked at him with her honey-colored eyes and for the first time since his colleague moved into the headquarters, their gazes held. The honey of Marta's eyes drew him in and he realized that she had an amber-colored ring right around her irises. The amber was mixed slightly into the honey making them look like an explosion had happened and the color splattered away. It was the first time Oliver had seen eyes like that. Such beautiful eyes.

Marta still maintained their eye contact, exploring the different sparkles and shimmers behind Oliver's green-blue eyes. Curiosity seemed to be the main emotion in his eyes but Marta also saw the depth of someone who had seen a lot of tragedy in his life hiding behind the smile on his face. His eyes gave him away. Oliver became more and more interesting to her. He seemed to be a man with many layers. A former SEAL, an Agent, a Christmas lover, smiling and handsome. A deep ocean and a ray of sunshine all at the same time. It had been years since Marta had had the urge to get to know someone. To get to know everything about them. Last time she ended up marrying the person. Frank.

Suddenly she broke away from Oliver's gaze, lowering her head and looking at the floor. She felt guilty for comparing Oliver to the love of her life. Especially on the day he'd died.

Oliver retrieved his hand from her upper arm, cleared his throat, and stepped towards the kitchen. Was it his fault that she looked so sad? Did he step over a line?

"I was just prepping the turkey for dinner. You want to help?" He asked, ignoring the sad vibes radiating from Marta.

"Turkey? Isn't that for Thanksgiving?" Marta asked, confused.

"Yeah, but we were on a mission during Thanksgiving and I didn't have turkey this year so I decided to do one today instead."

He beamed at her, his mouth literally drooling from thinking about the delicious food.

"I'm actually pretty good with turkey. My... my family always said I did the best one."

She rounded the kitchen counter to look at the large raw turkey resting on the countertop.

"Really? Go ahead then!"

Marta showed Oliver in great detail how she prepared the turkey before it went in the oven. It'd take a few hours, which left Oliver speechless. He hadn't made turkey on his own before and he'd expected it to be done within an hour.

"We have to baste it constantly so it doesn't become dry. Believe me, it'd taste awful then," she explained after they had placed the bird in the oven.

"I don't know about you, but I'm starving. I can't wait four hours 'til dinner," Oliver half whined, half chuckled.

"I'm hungry, too. What did you plan aside from the turkey?"

"Smashed potatoes and Brussels sprouts, but I won't be satisfied with just that..."

A loud sigh left Oliver's throat, and as if on cue, his stomach started to grumble.

"Nah, me neither," Marta sighed as well before they looked at each other and burst into laughter.

"Let's order some pizza! I'll call Butch and ask what he wants. I bet he's hungry, too, although he ate like half of the cookie dough when we were baking this morning."

"Oh wow. That's a lot of raw eggs. Hope he didn't have a stomach ache," Marta said, remembering an incident from when she was a child and ate a lot of cake batter.

"He's tough. Some raw eggs won't kill him," Oliver laughed before he started talking to Butch on his phone.

She couldn't hear what the other Agent was saying, but Oliver's responses made her think that Butch was laughing at the blond man.

"No, I didn't know it would take so long."

"No, I didn't buy a pre-cooked one."

"Stop saying that or you'll starve tonight."

"Yeah, I am being serious."

With a loud sigh he stopped the call before bursting into laughter and whispering "this guy" with a shake of his head.

"So?" Marta asked with a raised eyebrow.

"He insulted me and laughed at me for not knowing that a turkey needs more than a few minutes to cook. Oh, and he wants a pizza with ham and pineapple."

"Pineapple?" Marta looked at Oliver with shock all over her face.

"Yeah… He's… weird."

"That's not weird, that's disgusting!" Marta exclaimed a little too loudly.

"It's not disgusting, it's delicious."

A gravelly voice appeared behind her and Marta turned on her heel to see who was talking to her. She was surprised to see Butch enter the kitchen wearing black sweatpants and a black shirt. His hair was messy on top of his head and he looked like he'd just woken from a long nap.

"No, it's disgusting. Every Italian will agree with me," Marta huffed in his direction.

"Good thing I don't care about Italians then," Butch huffed, grabbing a bottle of sparkling water out of the fridge.

He was about to leave the kitchen again but suddenly stopped, alternating his gaze between Oliver and Marta and observed their Christmas sweaters with a frown on his face.

"Let me know when the pizza gets here. And Oliver?"

"Yes, pal?"

"Don't even think about giving me the sweater you bought. I won't wear it."

And with that, the brunette Agent left the kitchen again.

Marta wasn't sure what to think about that weird encounter so she only looked at Oliver with confusion. The blond man shrugged his shoulders, stepped to the couch, and grabbed a black sweater that was lying on it. He showed it to Marta and she could see a comic figure of Grumpy Cat on it and the words "Jingle all the way to hell" around it. She started to laugh, coughing a "very fitting" in between her shallow breaths.

"Right? I thought so, too. Too bad he won't wear it."

"We should make him wear it."

Oliver raised an eyebrow at Marta, not having any idea how the hell they would make his best friend wear the Grumpy Cat Christmas sweater.

"You paid for the pizza, right?" Marta started explaining.

"Yeah."

"So if he doesn't wear the sweater, he won't get his disgusting pineapple pizza. Easy win."

Oliver wasn't sure if that would work but it was worth a try so he agreed with Marta, placed the black sweater on the kitchen counter and started cleaning up the mess from their turkey preparation. He grabbed his phone and increased the volume of the Christmas playlist he was listening to. "Jingle Bell Rock" was currently playing and he started swaying his hips slightly to the beat of the song.

As they'd only prepared the turkey the mess was cleaned pretty quickly but Oliver turned up the music even more and stepped towards Marta.

"What are you doing?" she chuckled insecurely when Oliver grabbed her hand and pulled her towards the empty area between the dinner table and the couches.

"You owe me a dance!"

"I... what? When did you decide that?" Marta asked, confused, but instead of answering, Oliver only placed his other hand right above Marta's hip.

"I paid for your pizza as well. So you owe me a dance for it." The Agent winked at her the moment the song changed to a remix of "12 Days of Christmas".

Oliver started to move them together and Marta was totally overwhelmed with the whole situation, unsure if she should let go and enjoy the great evening with her colleague or run back to her room and hide for the rest of the day.

Today was a day of many emotions and her body wasn't sure which one was the strongest at the moment.

"Relax. It's only one dance, okay?" Oliver whispered at her, making them slowly spin around the living room.

With every step and every line of the song Marta indeed relaxed until she was finally fully enjoying the dance. She even started to sing the lyrics of the song with Oliver while grinning at him. Today she'd really found a new friend. Someone she enjoyed spending her time with. Someone who made her feel special.

When the song slowly subsided and they were waiting for the next one, they looked each other in the eyes, lips curled upward in a smile, but the moment Marta heard Mariah Carrey start to sing her song "All I want for Christmas is you", her face fell, tears gathered in her eyes, and she fought herself free from Oliver's hands.

The world was spinning around her, and waves of heat and cold spread throughout her body, while her hands started to shake.

The tears fell from her eyes, surprising Oliver who only looked at her with shock.

"Marta, are you okay?"

YOU DON' T HAVE TO TELL ME

December 24th, 2019

"I..." Marta stuttered, her body still shaking, and she wasn't able to answer Oliver.

The blond Agent stepped towards her, placing both of his palms on Marta's upper arms to steady the shaking woman.

"Marta. What's going on?"

"St-Stop. Stop that song," she said between clenched teeth, the tears still sliding down her cheeks.

Oliver immediately did as she requested but, even after a minute of silence in the room, Marta's condition didn't improve.

Oliver carefully guided her towards the nearest sofa, making sure she didn't collapse. He prepared himself to catch her just in case. Thankfully, she made it to the couch and immediately laid down on it with her feet slightly raised on the armrest. She closed her eyes, which alarmed Oliver.

"Marta?"

His voice was now filled with panic while he was looking around the room to check where he had left his phone a few minutes ago.

He could see it lying on the dinner table. He must have placed it there before Marta needed his full attention.

"Should I call an ambulance?" he asked her, his heart beating rapidly while multiple scenarios played out inside his head.

"No. No. I'm fine. Just give me a minute."

Hearing her voice and knowing that she hadn't collapsed gave him a little bit of relief but his shoulders remained tense. Marta's condition had changed so rapidly, from all smiling and dancing to almost collapsing within a second. Oliver didn't understand what the hell had happened. Did she have a heart attack? A seizure? It looked more like the panic attacks Butch suffered from when he had to go to the med-bay, but why would his colleague have a panic attack while dancing to Christmas music?

"Oliver?"

Marta's voice brought him back to reality and he realized he'd zoned out. He shook his head a little before looking into Marta's honey-colored eyes. There was a swirling vortex within them.

"Are you okay? Can I bring you something? Water maybe? Tea? A cookie?"

Oliver had started to ramble, finally being able to do something for her now that she was looking a little better.

"Oliver! Calm down. I'm fine."

It was now Marta's turn to calm *him* down, making sure he didn't run around the room like a headless chicken.

"I... Okay. But seriously, can I bring you some water?"

"Yeah. Water would be nice."

Marta forced herself to smile at him and she could practically see the tension ease from his shoulders. Oliver jumped back into the kitchen, opened the fridge, and got her a bottle of cold water. When he returned he still had a serious frown on his face but he looked more relieved than before. Marta was sitting now and took a big sip out the bottle while Oliver watched her like a hawk.

"Better?" He asked and gave her a smile.

"Yeah, thanks."

She saw the debate in his eyes to ask her why the hell her constitution had changed so fast but the internal battle took him way too long so Marta let out a loud sigh. She couldn't hide her past forever.

"That song...it...reminded me of something that happened exactly a year ago," the brunette woman started, tears filling her eyes again.

"You don't have to tell me if you don't feel comfortable. It's okay."

Oliver kneeled in front of the couch now, placing a hand on Marta's thigh, and started to draw indefinable shapes on them with the tip of his thumb.

It was so tender that the cracks in Marta's heart closed a little. The man in front of her radiated something that made her feel happy again. Made her feel like smiling, dancing, and laughing. Made her feel loved. Although he didn't really do anything, he was just there. Smiling at her, caressing his thumb over her thigh, but it was enough.

"No, it's okay. My therapist says I need to talk about it."

Marta patted the spot next to her on the couch but before Oliver could actually take his place, his phone rang. He looked at it and mouthed: "It's the guards. Bet that's the pizza."

He excused himself and quickly went to the main entrance to get their pizzas from the delivery man. On his way back to the kitchen he stopped off at Butch's room and gave him his pizza, complete with its weird topping.

"Are we eating in the kitchen together?" the brunette Agent asked, not sure which answer he'd prefer to hear.

"To be honest...." Oliver started, letting out a loud sigh, "... I think it's okay if you eat in your room. Marta and I are just chatting and babbling and I know you don't like making small talk."

He wasn't comfortable telling his best friend the truth. There'd be no way Marta would open up in front of a stranger and he felt they'd finally reached a point where they felt safe and comfortable sharing their stories with each other and he was really looking forward to that, no matter how dark Marta's would be. Butch raised an eyebrow, shrugged his shoulders, and mumbled an almost silent "okay" before closing the door in Oliver's face.

For a second the blond Agent felt guilty for excluding Butch from dinner. He knew how much his best friend struggled to be comfortable around people and today he suggested having dinner with Marta, someone he hadn't met that much over the last few months, but when Oliver had to decide between the well-being and comfort of his best friend or Marta he chose Marta without a second thought.

With his mind spiraling between the joy of having time alone with Marta, guilt for letting Butch stay in his room, and fear of whatever Marta was about to tell him, Oliver took his time to walk the few steps back to the kitchen. Balancing the two pizzas in one hand, he entered the room and looked around for Marta. She wasn't on the couch where he had left her but in front of the fridge instead. He heard her mumbling something but couldn't exactly understand what she was saying. Clearing his throat, he signaled to Marta that he was back and the brunette woman spun her head around to look at him, a shy smile on her face when she saw the large pizza boxes in his hand.

"You want a beer? We're out of wine but I definitely need some alcohol tonight."

"Sure. Beer and pizza sound like a great combo," Oliver smiled while placing the pizzas on the counter of the kitchen island.

He stepped around it and stopped in front of the cabinet that held the plates. Out of the corner of his eye he saw Marta's movement and suddenly she was standing right next to him with the two bottles in her hand.

"Do you need a glass?" she asked him in a low voice.

Oliver felt the hair on his neck rise while listening to the sound of her voice. It sounded so different than it usually did when she used that tone. He liked it.

"Nah, the bottle's fine," he answered before slowly opening the cabinet and grabbing two plates.

Marta was still glued in place next to him, a storm appearing within the honey of her eyes. She'd been ready to open up to him before his phone rang. Hell, she'd really wanted to, feeling that it might help her on her journey towards healing. Help her to move on with her life, because with Oliver she felt safe and happy after months of existing in darkness, grief, and solitude. She'd had to digest so many things over the past year, from losing her husband and unborn child to severe physical damage from her own wounds to the mental trauma that came with all of that. Being constantly terrified that someone would come after her again.

Perhaps talking to Oliver would help her reduce all the pressure on her shoulders. He had this calming vibe that she craved and it reminded her of Frank. Maybe that was why she was drawn to him the more he tried to lighten her mood.

"What did you order?"

Oliver's voice brought her back into the community kitchen, and she blinked a few times before stepping to where he was standing.

He'd opened both of the pizza boxes, looking at hers with a frown on his face.

"Bacon and mushrooms," Marta answered, but when Oliver looked at her with still furrowed eyebrows, she added, "Is something wrong with that?"

"No...no. Absolutely not. Just can't imagine that combo tastes good."

"You wanna try a slice?" Marta smiled at him.

"Don't know, to be honest," he chuckled.

"What did you order?"

"Chicken barbecue."

"Wow, Oliver. That's the most plain-ass order ever," Marta now laughed loudly, infecting Oliver with it.

"Is it?"

"Yeah, absolutely, but I like chicken barbecue. Can I have a slice of yours?"

The woman looked at him with puppy dog eyes, trying to convince him.

Oliver raised an eyebrow at her, drumming his index finger on his lips, and let out a long "Mhhhhmmmmm" as if he were giving her request some serious contemplation.

"Come oooooonnnn," Marta whined when Oliver didn't give her an answer right away.

"Why should I give you a slice of my plain-ass order when you can have your fancy mushroom pizza instead?" He asked her, his face still drawn into a weird grimace with his finger on his lips.

It looked adorable and Marta really struggled to not burst into laughter. Oliver really had a way of being hilarious by doing the smallest things.

"Because..." Marta started to think about the perfect argument, "...then you can try this masterpiece of taste as well. I'm willing to trade a slice of mine with a slice of yours." Her lips were pressed together, trying really hard not to smile, giggle or laugh.

"I don't think that's a fair trade. You gotta pay me something extra if you want me to try THIS."

He pointed at Marta's pizza.

"What do you have in mind?"

"You have to bake Christmas cookies with me tomorrow."

"But I thought you'd already done that today? How many cookies do you need?"

Marta looked at him, confused.

"As Butch ate most of the dough I actually don't have enough cookies to hand out to all our colleagues when they return on the 27th. I wanted to make small giftbags with home-made cookies for all of them as a welcome back," Oliver explained and Marta could see his eyes light up when he proudly told her about his idea.

"That's a super cute idea, Oliver," Marta smiled at him.

Did she just use the word *cute* in the same sentence as *Oliver*? Wow. This man really did something to her.

"Ah, it's nothing."

He waved his hand, giving her the widest smile as a reaction to her compliment.

"In that case, I'll bake cookies with you tomorrow but you have to give the pizza a serious chance."

"Deal!" Oliver exclaimed before placing a slice of each pizza on their plates.

He grabbed both of them before stepping toward the dinner table but Marta shook her head and pointed to the more comfortable couches instead. Pizza and couches sounded like the perfect combination on this very emotional and draining day.

Oliver grabbed the mushroom pizza first and gave Marta the side-eye before taking a bite with a loud huff. The woman watched him curiously, seeing his eyes widen as soon as the different tastes unfolded within his mouth.

"Wow," he commented, turning his head and shooting Marta a shocked glare.

"You didn't expect that, huh?" The woman laughed, taking a big bite of her own slice.

"No. Wow, it's brilliant. The saltiness of the bacon combined with the taste of the mushrooms. Great choice, Marta."

He bumped his shoulder into Marta's, as the Deputy Director grinned from ear to ear at his compliment.

After Marta was done with her second slice, her position changed drastically. Her shoulders hung low and Oliver could feel her taking deep breaths before she eventually cleared her throat.

"I still owe you an explanation," she started, her voice shaking a little as if she were about to cry again.

Oliver quickly placed his plate on the coffee table, turned his upper body towards her saying,

"You don't owe me anything."

"Oh, I do. You made me laugh and feel good today. On a day when all I wanted to do was curl into a ball underneath my blankets and cry myself to sleep. You really made my day today, Oliver and the least I can do is make you understand why I reacted the way I did when I heard that song."

She gave him a weak smile, tears glistering in her eyes again.

Oliver didn't know how to respond. Thankfully he didn't have to say anything because Marta changed her position on the couch a little so that she faced him, her legs crossed underneath her. Her shoulders were still hanging low as if the weight of the world were on top of them.

"Exactly a year ago my life was turned upside down. Literally."

A heavy sigh escaped Marta's mouth and the tears welled up on her eyeline until there were too many and a few spilled over and slid down her cheeks.

"I was a very active undercover Agent in the drug trafficking task force, Jakob was too. We blew up a lot of mafia groups that were dealing drugs by going undercover, gathering evidence, and then arresting them as soon as we had enough proof. For years I slipped in and out of different personas, infiltrating the underground world of Washington. And I was really good at my job. So good that I might have become a little reckless. I confused some of the background information for my last two undercover jobs. The mafia I was currently infiltrating became suspicious and they started to do some research and contacted other organizations. What I didn't know back then was that they found out that I was the mole."

"Oh shit," Oliver whispered, having a gut feeling about where Marta's story was heading.

"Yeah. Turned out the CIA didn't hide my personal information as well as they'd promised. They found us, me and my husband."

She needed to take a break, the tears were now streaming out of her eyes, forming small rivers across her skin.

She felt Oliver shift a little and he reached out his arm to touch and comfort her but, as she was facing him, he didn't know where to touch her so he placed his palm on her forearm that lay loosely in her lap.

"It was Christmas Eve and I wanted to bake some cookies for the next day. Yeah, funny, right? Same thing as you wanted to do with me today. Anyway, I returned home and heard a commotion from inside the house. When I entered and looked around for Frank I found him in our bedroom lying in a puddle of his own blood. He'd been shot."

The way her voice broke at the end of the sentence was enough for Oliver to scoot even closer to her, wrap his arms around her upper body, and pull her into a hug. Marta was startled by the unexpected movement but managed to wrap her arms around Oliver.

His scent reminded her of early morning walks in the forest. When the world started to come back to life after a long and dark night. Dew still on the leaves of the trees, the heavy scent of wood very present as the flowerheads were still closed because of the lack of sunshine over the night.

Marta took some deep breaths, each one calming her more until she was able to continue her story. Oliver held her close, trying to give her enough comfort so that she wouldn't break apart.

"He didn't have a chance. They shot him in the chest. Autopsy later confirmed the bullet grazed his heart and his aorta, so he bled out within seconds. I just hope it was fast enough that he wasn't in pain for too long."

Her sobs were muffled by Oliver's sweater. The Agent carefully caressed his hand up and down her spine, holding Marta's broken heart together with every touch of his fingers. He really had a healing aura.

"I am so sorry, Marta. I'm so sorry this happened to you," he whispered against her head.

The story shocked him deep into his core. To the very marrow of his bones. What this woman had experienced was something he wouldn't wish upon his greatest enemy. It was cruel, heartbreaking, and soul crushing.

"The mafioso was still in the house. He shot me in my shoulder and lower stomach. I lost the baby I was carrying."

Her shoulders shook even more intensely and Oliver's heart twisted in his chest.

Marta had been pregnant. She'd lost her husband and her baby within a few short minutes. How cruel could fate be to someone?

"I am so, so sorry," Oliver mumbled over and over, the hand that still caressed her back slightly shaking with the strength of his emotions. The last time he'd felt like that was after he'd found Butch in the hideout in Iraq and then again when the doctors told him about the massive amount of injuries his best friend had received.

"I thought I would die that day."

The sentence sent a shiver up Oliver's spine and he released Marta from his embrace. With a strong grip he held her shoulders in place and looked at her with a mixture of pity, sadness and happiness. It might have looked kind of creepy, but Marta didn't mind.

"But you didn't. And I'm very happy about that."

Marta gaped at him with shock on her face, and hadn't expected him to enjoy her company that much.

"But I didn't," she repeated.

"Marta, what happened to you is horrible. I can't even imagine how you feel about it. I'm so sorry that I annoyed you the whole day with bullshit like baking cookies and having dinner with me. I didn't know what an important day this was for you."

His eyes held tears of their own. Tears of guilt, tears that showed how much his heart broke for the woman in front of him.

"No. Don't be! I'm happy you distracted me today. Believe it or not, I really had a great day despite the circumstances. I…I just hadn't expected that song would bring back the trauma so heavily," she sighed.

"Why this song?" Oliver asked, confused, but Marta surely hadn't heard him as she was too lost in her thoughts, reliving the worst moments of her life.

"When I woke from the coma a few weeks later, a police officer told me that our neighbor heard the commotion and called the police. He saved my life. They arrived in time, just a minute after I was shot the second time. Because the neighbor reported that he had heard a gunshot, the emergency operator decided to send an ambulance as well. None of the bullets had hit a major artery so they were able to get me to a hospital in time. Of course I had lost a lot of blood and one of my ovaries as well as my colon were damaged, but in comparison to Frank...I was lucky. I thanked both of my heroes by buying them flowers. Ridiculous I know, in comparison to them saving my life, but I wanted to do something. I visited the emergency operator at work and gave her a big hug. Her name is Beckett and she had the warmest smile ever when I met her. She insisted she was just doing her job but for me she was a lifesaver. I wouldn't be here without her."

Oliver looked at her with pity. It still wasn't the explanation for the breakdown she had when she heard the song, but he was patient. He could give her all the time she needed to tell him about this horrible memory.

"The last thing I remember before I lost consciousness was that song and how awkwardly fitting it was to my situation," Marta sighed, but her eyes stayed dry this time.

She'd used up all her tears already. Oliver tilted his head a little, a painful grimace on his face.

"I'm so sorry," he said again, like a broken record, because that was actually all he could say.

He was a tumult of emotions but wasn't able to put them into words. Wasn't able to vocalize something that would make her feel better. Could take the pain from her. Because he knew he would never be able to.

"Sorry if that destroyed your Christmas mood," Marta sighed, a small smile creeping onto her face.

"Oh gosh, Marta. Don't care about my Christmas mood."

Oliver laughed because the whole situation was too fucked up to not to. He pulled her in for another hug, a tight one.

"I wish I could take that pain from you, but I know I can't. So I want you to know that I'm here for you. If you ever need a shoulder to lean on, someone to hold you while you cry as long as you need, or someone to lighten your mood when you feel sad, I'm here. I'll always be here. You shared your story with me and with that you let me into your life. And I refuse to leave it again. Sorry, not sorry."

Oliver's words were exactly what Marta needed to hear. They made her laugh. They were wholesome, assuring, but they also made her feel welcomed, comforted, and loved. Yes loved. Maybe on a different level than Frank loved her, but she was happy that she met Oliver and that he was very persistent in being a part of her life. She needed people like him around her.

"Thank you. I really appreciate that."

She gave him a smile, an honest one. One that even reached her eyes.

"Sure. You want more pizza?"

He rose from his position on the couch, grabbed both of their plates, and stepped towards the kitchen. The pizza might have been cold already, but it would still taste good.

"Yes, please. I'm actually starving!" She chuckled.

Oliver came back with loaded plates. With an amused look on her face, she could see another slice of his chicken barbecue pizza on her own plate. It was a sweet gesture. His way of showing her that he liked her and that he cared for her.

Both of them grabbed their slices before Oliver tried to clink them together like you would with glasses. Marta looked at him confused, but heard him say:

"Cheers to remembering your husband Frank today. Let's never forget him. And your baby. They made you who you are. They're a part of you. Let's never forget their part of you. Especially not today."

Marta had tears in her eyes again, but for a different reason now. She was touched. Touched by his big heart and wonderful words.

"But also cheers to everything that lies in front of me. I'm curious and excited about what it's gonna be," she whispered, seeing Oliver's eyes lit up.

"Cheers to that," he nodded.

For the rest of the night the smiles never faded from their faces. Despite the circumstances, it was a wonderful day. With good company.

In Oliver she had found a true friend. Someone she was happy having in her life. Her new life. She was still adjusting, but he was there, and he made her happy. That was definitely something worth exploring.

Comfort

NOW
June 2nd, 2022

It had been a rough day for all of them. Burying someone was never easy but the last two weeks had been a living hell for Marta and Oliver. Oliver's best friend Nate was mentally and physically destroyed and everything between him and his girlfriend, Lynn, was on the verge of collapsing. Lynn had joined the CIA at the beginning of the year as the CIA's resident doctor.

Alongside her regular job, patching up injured Agents, she'd decided to start helping Nate improve his PTSD. Oliver had been really grateful for her support, especially as it seemed like she was the only one who'd really made any progress with his best friend. With every passing week he saw more and more glimpses of his old best friend, the carefree, smiling man who was the most loyal friend he had ever known. That was until a terrorist took Nate hostage, tortured him for three months, breaking him in more ways than Oliver could ever imagine. After that, Nate suffered from PTSD every day until Lynn started to help him feel better.

For the last few months, Oliver's life had been almost perfect. His best friend didn't need his help every single day and he was finally dating the woman he'd loved for years. Every day felt like a blessing, but of course it was too good to be true.

A week ago they'd discovered that Lynn hadn't been entirely honest with them, a fact that had broken more than just Nate. Oliver and Marta had been just as devastated and there had been endless discussions about the situation and how they could have handled it. Instead of forcing them apart it had brought them even closer together than before. They'd both immediately agreed that they would have done the same as Lynn and were relieved that the situation wasn't going to drive a wedge between them.

Today they were mourning Lynn's sister Ann, who had been the biggest victim in this whole tragedy. She hadn't done anything to be involved in it but, in the end, she was the one to give her life. Not Lynn. Not Nate. And definitely not Oliver and Marta.

On a day like this nothing else mattered more than supporting each other to get through this day. Marta and Oliver were standing in the back, observing the interactions between Nate, Lynn, and Lynn's parents. Not many people from the Agency had come but, as none of them had actually known Ann, this wasn't surprising. She'd been nothing more than a chess piece in the cruel games of an insane terrorist. Even when az-Zawahiri lost his life at the end it felt like the CIA had been the true loser.

The sky was dark, blanketed by leaden clouds, while they watched the service take place. Watched Lynn fall apart with Nate by her side the entire time. Oliver was more than tense next to Marta, he had the urge to grab her hand or touch her back. Anything. Physical touch was his love language but, as their colleagues Tia and Birdie were standing right next to them, he couldn't risk it.

When the service was complete, all of their colleagues hurried to get out of the graveyard, expecting the heavens to open up any minute. But Marta hesitated, still standing in their spot under the huge oak tree.

"You okay, Sugar?" Oliver asked from the side, carefully placing his hand on Marta's lower back.

They were alone now, except for Nate, Lynn, and her family, who were having a discussion in front of Ann's grave.

"M'kay," Marta mumbled, but her words were anything but convincing.

Oliver let his hand slip down her back until it rested on her butt, his thumb drawing small shapes over it.

"Okay isn't enough for me. I wanna make you feel good. Let's head back to the compound."

Oliver leaned toward her, whispering the words in her ear.

The hairs on the back of Marta's neck rose with the thrill of his closeness but she couldn't give in to him yet. Although things between her and Oliver were amazing and she was pretty sure the whole mess around Lynn's incident would be sorted out soon, today had been an emotional day for her.

"I can't," she breathed, her eyes filling with tears, but she turned away from Oliver trying not to alarm him.

He hadn't done anything wrong and she didn't want him to feel bad.

"Hey..." he said as he gently grabbed her chin and turned her head towards him, watching the tears that gathered in her eyes with a concerned frown on his face.

"What's wrong, Sugar?"

His voice was like honey and able to make Marta feel comfort even in her saddest moments. It had been like that since the first day she met him.

"I need you to meet him," she blurted out, her voice thick with emotion.

"Who?" Oliver was confused, not having a clue what she was talking about.

Instead of answering him she grabbed his large hand in her small one and pulled him along through the graveyard. Oliver didn't say a word the entire time, he just let Marta pull him with her ridiculously strong arms. Sometimes he forgot what a bad-ass Agent she'd been and how hard she trained, although she complained the entire time that she hated working out. She was the personification of all bark and no bite when it came to exercise.

Suddenly their walk came to a halt and Oliver almost crashed into Marta as he hadn't realized that she'd stopped. He gazed around at the graves nearby until his eyes landed on the inscription of a large cross-shaped marble headstone right next to him:

Frank Gómez

Loving husband, wonderful son, amazing human

Taken suddenly and far too soon

We miss you. We love you.

"Oh," Oliver said, unsure what else was appropriate to say.

Instead of words he stepped up behind Marta, who had her body turned towards where her husband lay. He wrapped his arms around her middle, crossing them on her stomach, and rested his head on her shoulder.

"Oliver, this is Frank. Frank, this is Oliver," Marta whispered with a shaking voice.

"It's nice to meet you, Frank. Marta's told me so many amazing stories about you. I'm really sorry I was never able to meet you."

"You two would have got along pretty well. You have a lot in common."

"You think so?" He asked with a wistful smile.

"Yeah, pretty much."

They both fell silent. Marta's eyes were fixed on her husband's name, forever etched into the marble headstone, whilst Oliver had turned his head, leaning his forehead against her temple.

"Frank..." Marta's voice was slightly above a whisper and she radiated insecurity.

"... Oliver is my boyfriend. We've been dating for a couple of months now and I'm ready to take the next step with him. He's not you and he will never replace you. You'll have a place in my heart until I die, but he makes me happy. I wanted you to meet him because he's part of my life now."

Marta's words filled Oliver's heart, making it float out of his chest. Never in his life had someone said something so beautiful to or about him. Tears welled in his eyes as he placed a tender kiss on Marta's hair.

"I know you'd be happy for me because I'm finally able to move on. He made me do it. Oliver protects me, loves me, and makes me smile. That's all you ever wanted for me. I know that."

Finally Marta turned so that she was facing Oliver now.

Her boyfriend.

It still sounded weird in her head but she knew she'd get used to it.

"*Te quiero,*" Oliver whispered to her.

It was the first time he'd spoken Spanish to her and he'd chosen the most beautiful words but it wasn't just his words that reassured her that she'd made the right decision on giving him a chance. The look behind his green-blue eyes gave his feelings away. They were sparkling with love, pride, and adoration. And when she returned his gaze her eyes reflected those same emotions right back at him.

Back at headquarters, Marta and Oliver needed to be careful not to get caught by any other Agents but on their way from the main entrance to his room they couldn't keep their hands off each other. Their official label as boyfriend and girlfriend had them giggling like teenagers while linking their pinky fingers or placing a palm on the small of the other's back. Innocent, light, subtle touches but they meant the world to them.

On the elevator ride up to the first floor, Oliver risked pinching Marta's butt cheek, making her squeak a little, and the other people in the elevator turned around to look at them but both just looked straight ahead, smiling innocently at their colleagues as if nothing had happened. The moment the elevator doors closed behind them, Marta smacked her hand on Oliver's ass.

"You're such a bad boy," she said in a sultry whisper, looking around to make sure that no one else was in the hallway but thankfully they were alone.

"What do you want to do about it?" He teased quietly.

Marta's eyes widened when she heard his words, her tongue darting out to wet across her lips in anticipation. Instead of answering him, Marta crashed her lips into Oliver's, the force of her passion slamming his body against the wall. She placed both her hands on his hips, pinning him between her body and the wall. Oliver was taller and stronger than her, able to overpower her very easily if he wanted to, but he let her take all the control.

"I'm going to fuck this bad boy behavior out of you," she whispered against his lips before nipping gently at them.

Oliver groaned as his body flooded with pleasure. He'd always been the gentle type but on occasion Marta had been a little rougher than usual, taking charge, and he'd realized that he loved it, just as he loved every other part of her.

"Please," he replied, his voice rough with need.

"Give me your hand," Marta commanded, stretching out her own in expectation.

Oliver did as he was told and Marta hurried towards his room, pulling the blond Agent with her.

"What if Butch..." Oliver started to complain but stopped when he saw Marta's stern look.

"I don't care."

She dug her hand deep in the pocket of Oliver's pants, grazing her fingers along his cock, before pulling out the ID Card and opening the room. Oliver let out a loud groan, palming himself through the cloth as soon as Marta had turned her back to him.

What was this woman doing to him?

They entered his room and all Marta needed to do was point her index finger towards the bed to have Oliver eagerly comply with her unspoken order. He was surprised at the direction the afternoon had taken but if they were officially boyfriend and girlfriend then what a way to celebrate.

With slow, deliberate strides he walked towards the bed, turning around to look at Marta, ardently awaiting her next command.

"T-shirt off," she said imperiously while stepping in his direction.

Marta kept her distance watching intently as Oliver stripped out of his shirt and revealed the rock-hard abs beneath. She loved those abs, loved seeing them tense right before he climaxed. It was the best show she'd ever witnessed and she couldn't wait to see it again.

"Shoes and pants too."

Lust shimmered in Oliver's eyes when he watched Marta lean forward. He could see her dilated pupils in the light from the lamp. The fierce heat he saw within them melted any last bit of resistance he held and Oliver crumbled, willing to do anything for her.

After everything Marta had been through, to see this side of her, this *dominance* making its reappearance, was something that Oliver loved to see. And, as his hard cock could confirm, he loved her being in charge.

He opened the button and zipper on his pants, letting them slowly slide down his legs, maybe a little on purpose.

"What do you want me to do next?" He asked, his voice low and gravelly.

"Ma'am," she snapped.

"Pardon?" Oliver looked at her with a slightly tilted head in confusion.

"What do you want me to do next, *Ma'am*," Marta repeated pointedly.

That was new, but he liked it.

"Understood?" Marta asked, her voice a sharp whisper.

It was the sexiest it had ever sounded and Oliver felt himself growing even harder at the sound.

"Yes, Ma'am," he repeated.

"Good boy."

A groan left his throat and he nearly dropped to his knees before her. Marta had successfully unlocked a new kink in him.

"Lie on the bed, on your back," she commanded and Oliver followed without wasting another second. Instead of following him as he'd expected, she made her way to his closet and began digging through one of the drawers that he used for workout clothes.

"What are you..."

"*Sin hablar*. Quiet."

This time her voice was sharper, commanding, and strict. It was her Deputy Director's voice, shouting orders around every day. He followed her order, watching her intensely and with curiosity. What was she looking for?

"We aren't going to do anything weird, I promise, but I want you to know that I'll stop if you want me to, okay *mi cielo*?" Oliver nodded.

Marta had turned around now, two ropes in her hands.

"Where...?"

"I bought them and stored them here. Was wondering if you'd find them."

She smiled at him, something playful shimmering in her eyes. Oliver propped himself up on his elbows, looking at Marta with a smirk.

"I didn't."

"No. But you'll find out very soon what we're going to do with them."

She made her way over to the bed, her hips swaying as she walked. Standing next to it, she leaned down to place a kiss on Oliver's lips. He reached out his hands to touch her, but she clicked her tongue and grabbed his large hand with one of hers.

"No touching."

"But..."

"I *said* no touching, *cariño*."

Marta's voice was still low and the tone of it, with that slight commanding rasp, made Oliver tremble. He reached down to stroke himself through his boxers, but Marta grabbed his other hand as well.

"I said no touching. Not me. Not yourself. I promised to fuck this bad boy attitude out of you, and that is exactly what I'm going to do."

Oliver groaned in response as an electric thrill ran down his spine. He'd never done anything like this before, taken things as far as this, but he didn't want to stop.

"Understood?"

Marta had both of his hands in a strong grip while leaning down and hovering her head above his.

"Yes, Ma'am," Oliver whispered, the urge to shoot up and connect his lips with hers almost overwhelming but he resisted, not wanting to feel the sting of her disappointment.

"*Bueno.* Good boy," she purred and his heart sang at the praise.

She let go of one of his hands and started to wrap the rope around it, before tying it in an easy knot.

"Is this okay?"

She had locked her eyes with him, making sure he was truly comfortable.

"Yes, Ma'am," he insisted.

His answer must have reassured her, Marta gave him a small wink before turning her attention to the headboard. It was only one flat board that was covered in fabric. When she'd bought the ropes she had thought about her own bed which had wooden pillars at the end of the headboard. Perfect to tie ropes around it.

But here? Impossible.

Her face fell, the badass attitude gone, while everything she had planned for today crumbled to pieces in front of her.

Oliver saw it, concerned about her abrupt change in emotions, but before he was able to say something, Marta regained her posture and rolled her shoulders. Symbolizing that she was jumping back into the role she wanted to play today.

Taking Oliver's other hand, she wrapped the end of the rope around it so that both his hands were fixed together. Oliver gave her a nod, signaling that he was okay with the tightness of the rope. She grabbed his now-bound hands and pinned them above his head.

"I want you to leave your hands there. No touching. *Bien*?"

"Yes, Ma'am," he eagerly nodded.

Marta placed her hand on Oliver's cheek, brushing her thumb over it, and smiled at him.

"If you say stop, I'll stop immediately and get this rope off your hands."

"I'm okay, Sugar," Oliver smiled and Marta ignored the fact that he had called her by his regular pet name.

Marta stepped to the end of the bed, turning towards Oliver and started to slowly strip off her clothes. The t-shirt, shoes, socks, and jeans until she was standing in front of him in her underwear. White panties and a black bra. Not matching, but neither Oliver nor she cared. No woman wears freaking matching underwear every day. It's just not realistic.

"You are *so* beautiful," Oliver whispered, his eyes dropping down to her covered breasts multiple times.

The bulge in his boxers twitched and when Marta slowly reached behind her back to open her bra, she heard him let out a little moan. The moment his eyes saw her nipples he couldn't help it anymore. His tied hands drifted to his crotch and he stroked along his cock.

A stinging pain shot through his thigh and he gasped. Marta had slapped her palm on it with so much force that he still felt the pain pulsating and he was sure he'd see the outline of her hand on it tomorrow.

"I said no touching. Is that so hard to understand, Agent?" She said roughly.

"Sorry, Ma'am," Oliver hissed, the pain in his thigh still very present.

He placed his hands above his head again, watching the angry expression on Marta's face. He saw a short flicker on her face, worried she may have hit him too hard, but it was gone within a second when she saw he was fine.

Slowly she climbed on the bed, crawling up to him until her head reached his hips. Marta lowered her head and kissed along the outlines of Oliver's cock, still covered by his boxers. She heard his hungry moans, before she hooked her teeth around the top of his boxers and pulled them down his legs. His shaft sprang free, rock hard and ready for Marta to use. He wasn't thick, but long. Longer than every other man she'd sex with before, but it was the perfect length, reaching the spot of ultimate pleasure within her with ease.

Marta started to lick along his shaft, the tip of her tongue traveling the path of the vein that ran along his length. Oliver was a moaning mess underneath her tongue even though she'd only just started. When she reached the tip of his cock she carefully wrapped her mouth around it and flicked her tongue around the tip. Oliver grabbed the pillow between his still tied hands, the urge to hold onto something strong within his body. His eyes were closed, his head pressed back into the mattress.

"Oh God," he moaned when Marta took his cock down her throat a few times but suddenly he felt the warmth around his cock disappear. He opened his eyes and looked at Marta in surprise.

She'd changed her position a little, resting on one of his thighs while looking up at him with fire in her eyes.

"Quiet, or your best friend will hear how I work you until all you can do is whimper. You don't want him to ask weird questions, do you?"

Oliver shook his head. Getting weird comments from Nate about him overhearing their sex play was the last thing he wanted.

"Can you be quiet for me then, *mi cielo*?" she crooned.

"Yes, Ma'am."

"That's my good boy."

With that Marta lowered her head again, wrapped her gorgeous lips around his cock once more and sucked him deeply. Oliver bit his lips to prevent himself from moaning and thankfully it worked. The tension in Marta's own body was unbearable and she felt herself soaking Oliver's thigh. She needed some sort of release so while she was bobbing her mouth up and down Oliver's shaft, she started to circle her hips along his thigh, putting the perfect pressure on her clit to keep herself on the edge.

Oliver couldn't hold back his moans anymore, his lower lip was already almost bleeding from the pressure of his teeth but the moment the moans became louder, Marta stopped again. The Agent groaned in frustration. She'd worked him close to the edge and he knew he only needed a little bit more to fall apart.

Marta rose from the bed, stood in front of the closet again, and grabbed a pair of socks. Oliver looked at her with a raised eyebrow, his mind still fuzzy from the pleasure and the blood that had obviously wandered down into his shaft. She was suddenly standing next to his head, sliding her panties down her hips until she held them in one and the socks in the other hand.

"One is for a *good* boy, the other for a *bad* one. Which one are you going to be today, *mi cielo*?"

"I'm a good boy for you, Ma'am."

"Open your mouth."

Oliver didn't even think about what she was going to do, he only followed her order until the socks were filling his mouth almost completely, muffling whatever would slip out of his throat.

"If you can't be quiet, I need to make you," she winked before crawling back on top of him.

Marta rested her hips on top of Oliver's thighs, grabbing his cock in her hand and giving him a few strokes to test the improvised gag. She could hear him make some muffled noises but they were too quiet for Nate to hear them through the wall. It was perfect.

One of her hands worked on his cock, while her other wandered down to her clit and started to circle it. She was already wet and ready for him but she wanted to build up that tension a little more. Oliver tried to leave his eyes open to watch Marta working on herself but the pleasure of the whole situation overwhelmed him, forcing him to shut his eyes and press his head into the mattress. He was a moaning, needy mess.

"Now, I'm going to ride you and if you carry on being a good boy for me I might even let you come."

Oliver was only able to nod, his eyes open just a slit while he watched his girlfriend hover over his cock and line him up with her entrance. When she let herself sink down on him, they both moaned in harmony. Oliver filled her so perfectly and when he bottomed out she stilled, enjoying the feeling a little longer. The tip of his cock reached that spongy spot inside of her that she knew would bring her a phenomenal orgasm and so she started to move her body up and down his shaft. A never-ending symphony of muffled moans came out of Oliver's mouth while he gave in to Marta riding his cock.

The tension within Marta's body intensified fast, the whole feel of him giving her body pleasure. She placed her hands on Oliver's chest, steadying her body while still bobbing up and down his shaft. Her head rolled on her neck, her eyes closed, and she struggled to keep her own moans quiet. But when Oliver started to buck his hips, pounding into her from below as deep as he could get, the knot in her lower stomach exploded, and she tumbled over the edge while screaming his name.

So much for being quiet.

Oliver felt her walls clench around him and it was all he needed to spill deep into her with a muffled groan. Marta managed to move a little longer before she felt him slowly soften inside of her and she stopped the movement. Her arms were trembling, and her breath was shallow as she panted heavily. She gripped into his chest with so much force that her fingernails left crimson crescents all around his muscular chest. She kept him inside of her while leaning forward and grabbing the socks from Oliver's mouth to place a loving kiss on his lips.

"That. Was. Phenomenal," he whispered to her in between kisses.

"I agree."

She smiled at him before hurrying to the bathroom and soaking a flannel with warm water to clean them both. Oliver's hands were still tied together, so she took her time for aftercare, washing away the evidence of their sexual activities from his body before she started to clean herself. Then she carefully freed him from the rope and collapsed on the bed next to him.

Oliver turned to his side, faced Marta, and placed his large arm over her stomach.

"I liked that a lot, you in charge. We should do that more often," he whispered before placing kisses along her shoulder.

"Yeah? Wasn't it too much?" Her voice sounded insecure, completely different than a few minutes ago.

"No, it was totally fine. I liked the adrenaline mixed with pleasure. That's a combination I've never felt like this before, but it was amazing."

"Okay, good."

She had turned her head around and smiled at him, exhaustion visible in her eyes. She'd done the majority of the work so it was totally understandable that she was tired.

"Although I have to admit that the quiet thing didn't really work," Oliver giggled, remembering her screaming his name so loudly that he was pretty sure the entire hallway had heard.

"Yeah. I couldn't control myself. You felt too good inside me," Marta chuckled herself.

They snuggled into each other, ready to fall asleep arm in arm. Oliver leaned his forehead on Marta's shoulder and she could feel his breaths become more with every passing second.

"Hey boyfriend?" She whispered, getting a "Mhm" from Oliver as response.

"Thank you for bringing me this comfort. I love you."

"I love you, too."

And with that they both drifted off from their highs into a sex-induced sleep, a smile dancing around both their lips.

WELCOME TO THE FRIENDZONE

THEN
Summer 2021

"You wanna have the special McGreen lasagna for dinner?"

Oliver popped his head into Marta's office, a wide grin on his face, his eyes sparkling with excitement. Over the past few months he and Marta had become good friends, enjoying their evenings together while cooking, watching movies, or playing board games. It hadn't been anything fancy, as Marta refused to leave the headquarters, but they tried their best to keep themselves entertained.

"Sounds amazing! Gotta get some paperwork done before but I think I'll come downstairs to you in about an hour. That okay?"

She smiled back at him, her stomach already grumbling in anticipation of a delicious dinner.

"Okay but I'm starving so I'm giving you an hour or I'll start without you."

"You wouldn't dare!" Marta exclaimed, her eyes wide and her mouth open in a theatrically shocked expression.

"Oh yes, I would."

Oliver winked at her and then his head was gone from the doorframe. Marta shook her head, but a warm smile remained on her face.

Exactly 55 minutes later she entered the community kitchen to find Oliver already opening a bottle of red wine.

"I thought you said you'd wait for me," she spoke into the room, making Oliver jump from where he was currently standing.

"Holy shit, I almost spilled the entire bottle of wine. Imagine that!"

"That would've been a tragedy. I can't stand having an evening with you without being drunk."

Marta winked at him before stepping towards the kitchen island and slapping her palms on the cold surface.

Instead of answering her Oliver placed one of his hands above his heart, his face furrowed in pain to show her that her statement had hurt him.

"Stop messing around and start making dinner. You really don't want to see me hangry," Marta threatened, rounding the island and silently offering her help.

"Yes Ma'am," he answered before grabbing a large pan and a casserole dish out of the cabinet next to the stove.

Marta quickly shook her head and tried to ignore the rising heat in her lower belly after hearing what he had called her.

"What can I do?"

"You can cut the onions and celery and peel the carrots."

Marta raised an eyebrow at him before she asked "Carrots? Celery?"

She heard Oliver chuckle while he put oil in the pan and started to sauté the ground beef.

"My mom used lasagna to get Simon and me to eat some veggies. We hated veggies so she smuggled carrots and celery into the sauce. We never realized it until I asked her for the recipe when I moved out."

"Your mom is a very clever woman," Marta commented, carefully cutting the onions, which wasn't easy as her eyes began to water.

"That she is."

"So you have a brother?"

Marta tried to keep the conversation alive, not that it was hard talking to Oliver. They had great chemistry and talking to each other felt just natural but he barely spoke about his family so she tried to dive deeper into that topic.

"Yeah."

He was unusually uncommunicative about it, which made Marta curious.

"You two are close?"

"Nah. We used to be as kids and teenagers but the SEALs separated us."

"How come?"

Oliver didn't answer immediately, focusing on pushing the ground beef around the pan. Marta could almost hear him searching for the right words. She gave him all the time he needed, knowing well that pushing it wouldn't be the right thing to do.

"My parents made the mistake of treating us very differently for our life choices," he started before falling silent again.

He was struggling with all the long-buried emotions coming back to the surface.

"My brother was a genius in school, got a scholarship for studying business, and quickly made his way into a company that sold computer software. He got promoted a lot, has a great salary, and lives in a big house. Simon really has an amazing life and I'm happy for him, really."

"Wow, that sounds like a great career. Your parents must be very proud of him," Marta commented, worried about the appropriateness of her comment after Oliver had said that the two brothers were estranged.

"Yeah, they should be but instead they took it for granted that he achieved everything with flying colors. He got the occasional clap on the shoulder and a hug from Mom, but he never got what I got, the true appreciation."

Marta heard him sigh loudly before he grabbed the onions and put them in the pan with the ground beef. Then he turned around to preheat the oven. He was obviously stalling so he didn't have to continue the story.

"That sucks," Marta commented.

She was done with the veggies so all she could do was watch Oliver do literally anything to distract him from their conversation.

"Yeah. After the Bin Laden operation things got out of hand. When I got the medal of honor they were so proud, telling everyone about me and what I achieved while forgetting that they had another son. Simon was super pissed and I can understand why. He worked so hard all those years to achieve what he had and our parents totally ignored him. For months they only shared their love with the son that killed Osama Bin Laden."

"Now I know why your name is so familiar. You were the SEAL that killed Bin Laden!" Marta exclaimed loudly but regretted it immediately.

It had totally destroyed the vibe and atmosphere between them. She quickly mumbled a "Sorry" and waited for him to continue the story.

"That was actually the worst time for me. The military and press wanted me to celebrate this success, taking pictures of me everywhere and asking me for interviews and all that stuff but I was mourning my best friend and nobody cared about that."

"Oh, I didn't know that your friend was killed in that operation. I'm so sorry to hear that."

Marta placed her palm on Oliver's upper arm, who was still pushing the ingredients around the pan in front of him. His gaze was lowered, she couldn't look him in the eyes.

"Butch wasn't killed in that operation. He was kidnapped, but there were no hints of where they took him so the military declared him killed in action after a few days."

Marta's eyes widened when things became more clear in her mind. Butch had been Oliver's friend for a very long time and she knew that his nickname "Butch" came from his SEAL name "The Butcher". Oliver's comments about Nate going through a lot made more sense for her now too. The man had been kidnapped and everybody thought he was dead and still he was walking through headquarters.

"It became even worse in the months after the initial operation. It was a miracle but we found Butch. Alive. Well, mostly alive. He had a lot of injuries and it was touch and go for a few weeks but he survived the whole thing. I had my best friend back at least, I thought so, but Butch came back a different person. The man you know now; the grump, the lone wolf. He wasn't like that before the kidnapping. I don't know exactly what happened to him, he still refuses to talk about it, but I knew I needed to be there for him. I was the only one able to calm him after the coma and I wanted to help him get back on his feet as best as

I could. It meant I didn't visit my family as frequently as before. My parents didn't mind, telling me I had more important things to do, but Simon was furious that my parents still saw me as their favorite, even though I left them hanging almost the entire time. Butch was my priority. I lost him once and I didn't want to lose him a second time."

Instead of responding with words that wouldn't have any effect on Oliver's broken heart, Marta stepped even closer and let her hand caress along his spine in a desperate attempt to comfort him.

Oliver turned around and Marta saw for the first time that he was crying. His eyes were puffy and red, with tears still slipping out of them from time to time. Her heart ached and she pulled on his arm to pull him in for a hug. The taller Agent let her wrap her arms around his middle and felt himself giving into her. His heart was beating fast, he enjoyed the coconut scent of Marta's hair and the grief seemed to leave his body as soon as she hugged him close to her.

"You are such an amazing human Oliver, I hope you know that," she mumbled into his chest, snuggling her nose even a little deeper.

Although technically she was hugging him it felt good to be in his arms and she hadn't felt that good in a long time.

"I don't know about that," Oliver mumbled and Marta slapped his back a few times.

"Don't say that. You're amazing. You'd better start believing it or I'll punch it into you."

Her words made Oliver chuckle before they stepped apart.

"I mean it. None of what happened is your fault. That your parents behaved that way, or that Butch had this traumatic experience. None. Okay?"

"Mhm."

"Oliver."

"Yeah, okay."

It was very obvious that he didn't believe his own words, but it was enough for Marta.

For now.

"This one operation separated our family and I feel very guilty for it, even though it wasn't my fault. My parents made a big mistake but it took them years to realize that and by then it was too late. Simon and I only talk to each other on birthdays and Christmas now, that's it."

"Listen to yourself. It. Is. Not. Your. Fault. Okay?"

Marta placed her hands on each of Oliver's forearms, almost begging him to finally believe her.

Her heart ached for him because she couldn't stand seeing her personal sunshine be sad. Oliver had this magical way of making her feel good, making her smile and laugh, and he had been by her side after Frank died. Now it was time for her to return some comfort, but he didn't let her.

"You're a loyal friend, you do an amazing job, and you're an amazing human being, Oliver. I haven't felt this good around someone since..."

She swallowed the lump in her throat.

Oliver understood what she meant and she could see a small smile dancing across his lips. It was a huge compliment and his heart burned when he realized how hard it must have been for Marta to vocalize these feelings. It meant the world to him.

"Thank you," he whispered, pulling her in for another hug.

His nose was buried deep in her hair, his arms strong around her shoulder holding her as close as possible. He couldn't deny that Marta made his heart skip a beat and that he wanted to be around her as much as possible. He even caught himself smiling every time he saw her cross his path. If it was during meetings or when he saw her walking the hallways no matter how many people were between him and her he was able to fix his gaze on her every time. Like his eyes were meant to look at her and, although she'd said that he made her life better, she didn't realize how much she helped him too. For years he'd been drowning in sorrow for the mental state of his best friend, constantly feeling guilty that Nate had to suffer.

He still felt guilty but, now he had Marta around, Nate was not the primary topic occupying his brain anymore. Oliver finally had something he could look forward to; cooking with Marta, watching movies, or playing board games. He couldn't wait for his day to be over so he could spend time alone with this wonderful woman.

And suddenly Oliver realized that he had fallen in love with Marta.

He pulled her even closer, closed his own eyes, and enjoyed the moment with her. Her face was buried in his neck and he felt her breath on his skin, leaving goosebumps. Marta was still trying to comfort him so she carefully let her hand caress up and down his back. Every time her fingertips touched his shirt, Oliver's skin burned. This woman was driving him crazy and he couldn't understand why he hadn't realized before that they were more than just friends.

When they broke apart, he quickly placed his palms on both of her cheeks, smiling at her with sparkles in his eyes. Marta was confused and taken by surprise and her eyes widened slightly.

"What are you doing?" She asked, a slight shaking in her voice clearly audible.

"You trust me?"

"I do."

"Then promise me that whatever happens now, you won't hate me."

"I don't know if I can do that," she chuckled slightly, the joke helping her to cope with the insecurity and fear the whole situation brought to her heart.

"Marta..."

"Okay, okay. I promise."

He could hear the slight sigh.

Oliver's thumbs caressed over her hot and blushed cheeks before he slowly leaned in and hovered his lips over hers. His green-blue eyes fixed on her honey-colored ones the entire time looking for hesitation or panic but all he could see was confusion and a storm whirling behind the honey of her eyes.

It was enough for him to finally close the gap and when his lips touched hers they were two puzzle pieces that finally found their way to each other. Butterflies appeared in his stomach, his heart drummed beneath his rib cage and he could hear her every heartbeat.

This was how it was meant to be.

Marta was surprised that she felt exactly the same: the butterflies, the heat, and the increased heart rate. It was all there. She parted her lips slightly to give his tongue access allowing him to explore. His tip gently touched hers and fireworks exploded in her lower bell, a feeling that she thought she'd buried with Frank a long time ago.

It had taken Oliver only a single kiss to bring it back to the surface and Marta had to admit that she hadn't felt so good in a long time. His featherlight brushes over her cheeks made her blush even more while her eyes remained closed. Their tongues danced around each other, exploring the sensations between them.

It was so right but so wrong at the same time.

They broke apart to catch a breath and when she opened her eyes again she could see Oliver smile widely.

But Marta didn't smile.

She felt phenomenal. Better than she had felt in the last months, but she didn't want to feel like that. It felt wrong.

"I can't," she mumbled, tears gathering in her eyes.

"What do you mean?" He asked, confused.

Oliver leaned back a little to look her in the eyes and when he saw the tears in them, his eyebrows furrowed in pain. He hated seeing her like that, especially after he had kissed her.

"I can't. It's not right."

"Did it feel bad for you?"

"No... it..."

But Marta couldn't find the right words to describe it.

The emotions were overwhelming her. Love, guilt, sadness, grief, and happiness. This combination didn't feel right, and it wasn't. She shouldn't feel like that after such an amazing kiss.

"I don't understand," Oliver whispered and she saw the confusion dominate his expression.

"You're my best friend. I can't."

"And you're one of my best friends. But that doesn't mean that we can't be a couple, can't explore the feelings between us. Come on, Marta, you can't tell me that you don't feel the same," Oliver pleaded.

It sounded more desperate than he'd wanted it to be but he'd always been bad at hiding his feelings.

"You're my best friend," Marta repeated a few times.

Oliver sighed, knowing that he had lost her to the rabbit hole of her mind.

"Marta..." he began, but her repetitive mumble didn't give him a chance to really reach her.

Instead of talking to her he grabbed her face a little tighter without actually hurting her. His thumbs started to draw circles on her cheeks again and the moment he saw her finally look at him properly, he spoke.

"There you are."

A wide smile was on his face once more although his heart felt like it was made out of ice. Her reaction had hurt him a lot but he saw that she was struggling with the kiss way more than he was. And he was the one who'd initiated it, so he felt guilty for confusing her. He knew what she'd been through with Frank and that she'd probably never be ready to love someone again.

But still, here he was, kissing her out of nowhere.

Overwhelming her.

Oliver felt incredibly guilty.

"I'm sorry, Marta, I shouldn't have done that."

He pulled his hands back, stepping away from her to give her some privacy.

She looked at him, still confused and shocked.

"Oliver..." she mumbled, her eyes filled with tears again.

"No, it's okay. I'm so sorry. That was a stupid idea. I thought you'd feel the same but that's obviously not the case. I'm so sorry. Please don't hate me now."

Tears started to form in the corner of his eyes and Marta stepped closer to him while placing one of her hands on his waist.

"I do feel the same, but I can't. It's okay that you kissed me. In a different world, in a different universe, this would have been perfect. But I can't. I don't hate you. You're still my best friend."

That was enough to let the tears fall down Oliver's face and he turned his head to the side so that she wouldn't see them. She quickly grabbed his chin and turned his face back towards her.

"I am sorry," he whispered.

"Oliver McGreen," Marta said with a stern voice, letting Oliver's eyes widen slightly while he looked at her with furrowed brows.

"You don't have to be sorry. It's all okay. We're good."

"You don't hate me?"

"No, I don't hate you."

His features softened and he looked relieved.

"Are you still my friend?" His voice was small, as if he were scared to speak the words out loud.

"Of course, Oliver. You're still my best friend. Let's pretend this never happened, okay?"

She shot him a shy smile.

"Okay."

Deep in his heart he didn't want to pretend that this never happened. Marta had parked him in the friendzone after she confessed she felt the same way but still she kept him at arm's length and didn't want him to be close.

What should he do?

Kiss her again?

Forget that it happened even once?

His heart was bleeding because of the rejection although he was relieved that he hadn't lost her.

A burning sensation in his heart made one thing very clear for him:

He'd fight to get out of the friendzone.

I DON' T WANT TO LOSE YOU

THEN
Fall 2021

"Come on, go on a date with me," Oliver begged.

"You know how ridiculous that sounds, right?"

"It's not ridiculous. I just really want to go on a date with you. You can't deny the chemistry between us, Marta. The longer you do it, the more depressed you're gonna be when you're finally ready and I'm off the market."

Instead of taking his argument seriously Marta burst into laughter. They were sitting on the couch in the community kitchen, a bowl full of popcorn on Marta's lap, while watching the animated version of "Arielle" on the big TV in front of them.

"Why are you laughing?"

Oliver looked at her, in surprise. It wasn't exactly the reaction he'd expected.

"You've barely been going out because you've been babysitting Butch for ten years now. When would you even meet another woman? Don't get me wrong, you're a handsome, funny, and charismatic guy, but that doesn't mean anything when you can't show it to someone."

She clapped her palm on Oliver's thigh before grabbing a big handful of popcorn.

"That's pretty mean, you know that?"

"Yeah."

"Seriously Marta..."

Oliver grabbed the remote control and paused the movie, getting a loud sigh in response.

He shifted his body a little so that he was facing Marta before grabbing the bowl of popcorn off her lap to place it on the coffee table. She knew what was coming: another big speech from Oliver to convince her to go on a date with him.

Did she like him? Sure.

More than friends? Maybe.

But there was no way she could date him. Her heart was not ready.

"Why are you denying that there's something between us?" He continued, his voice full of pain.

She knew it hurt him every time she declined his request and of course she was scared that someday he wouldn't be able to be her friend anymore.

"I'm not denying it," she mumbled, her gaze fixed on her legs.

She had switched to sitting cross-legged so that she was easily able to face him as well.

"So you feel it, too? That there's more between us? I'm pulled towards you as soon as you step into a room. Your laughter sets my heart on fire and every time you touch me I feel like I'm flying. You do things to me, Marta, that no one else has done before and I know that I'm in love with you."

It was the first time he'd actually spoken out loud about what had been building between them for months. The mutual attraction had been very obvious. Of course Marta felt it too, it was hard not to. Oliver made her happy and she longed to lay in his arms while they watched a movie. When he caressed his fingers over her shoulder fireworks exploded under her skin.

Only one other man had made her feel like that before and he was the reason she wasn't able to enjoy this growing relationship between her and Oliver.

Frank hovered above them constantly, his ghost a lingering presence in the back of Marta's mind.

"Oliver..." she started but didn't have a chance to continue as the blond Agent grabbed one of her hands and held it tight within his own.

"No. Don't bullshit me again with some kind of lame excuse. You and I feel the same so why the hell are you not able to say yes to a simple fucking date?"

He was angry, he was hurt, and he had every right to be. She constantly gave him mixed signals and it wasn't fair of her. Of course she enjoyed the intimacy between them. Cooking, joking, cuddling. It was all she yearned for after a shitty work day when one task force messed up badly.

His scent was the only thing that calmed her down these days, but on the other hand she was holding him at arm's length when it came to other things like dating, kissing, or even sex.

She wasn't ready for this but even if she was, she simply couldn't. It wasn't possible.

"We're not allowed to," she said, referring to their positions within the CIA.

She was his boss, his direct commander. He had to obey her orders, whether he liked them or not. The two of them dating would blur the boundaries between private life and work life and it could lead to problems on operations.

"For fuck's sake!" Oliver snapped, jumping to his feet and stalking around the room in an effort to calm his raging thoughts so that he could have a normal conversation with her.

"But it's true."

"Of course it's true, Marta, but when have you cared about rules from HR? You're literally known for not giving a shit about HR. Gary has a picture of you on his dart board in their break room," Oliver snarled, his mind recalling the moment he discovered that Gary indeed saw Marta as the worst.

"This is different," she protested, but her voice wasn't really convincing.

"How is that different, huh? Different from sending Agents back home in the middle of their shifts because they just lost a team member and can't concentrate on filling out mission reports? Different from sending Agents undercover in order to burst a drug trafficking ring even though HR hadn't given their permission yet?"

"We needed to be fast, HR didn't understand that."

"That's not the point," he groaned, his hands in front of his face while shaking his head intensely.

This woman drove him nuts. Sometimes in a good way and sometimes not.

"Oliver..." she tried, but again he interrupted her. She'd never seen him so angry.

"No. Don't *Oliver* me with that fucking angelic voice of yours. I'm done. I'm spent. We have amazing chemistry, we love each other, and we work well together. For fuck's sake, just give me one damn chance to prove to you that I'd be a good catch."

He stood in the middle of the room, almost screaming every word at her. Angry tears gathered in his eyes whilst his heart bled. Scared to hear yet another denial.

Slowly Marta rose to her feet, stepped in front of Oliver, and placed her hands on his forearms.

"May I say something now?"

She gave him a weak smile, carefully caressing her finger over his hairy forearms.

He didn't answer, giving her silent permission to continue.

"First of all, you would be an amazing catch. Whoever gets you as her boyfriend one day is one damn lucky bitch."

Oliver chuckled at her choice of words, mimicking his cursing from before.

"I can't deny the chemistry between us. You're my best friend."

The man in front of her groaned, hating the last two words more than anything else. He didn't want to be her best friend.

"You might even be more," she quickly added, letting his eyes slightly widen, and a sparkle appeared in them.

Was this it? Was she finally allowing him to date her?

"But I can't date you. It's not possible. I like you more than I care to confess. I'd even call it love. I dare you to even try to say something now."

Oliver's mouth had dropped open at the point of her confessing her love to him but he closed it as soon as he heard her words and felt her index finger prod into his chest. Instead both of them only looked into each other's eyes, taking deep breaths. Oliver was the first one to break the silence.

"But why? I don't understand it. I love you, you love me. We're more than just dating, we're fucking confessing our feelings, Marta."

"I know."

"Then explain it to me. It doesn't make any sense."

"I don't want to lose you," she blurted out, the tears she had tried so hard to hold back falling down her cheeks.

Instinctively, Oliver grabbed her into a tight hug, pressing her face into his chest. He could smell the coconut in her shampoo as he snuggled his nose deep inside the messy and curly brown hair.

"You won't lose me," he mumbled, pulling her even closer and rubbing his hand along her spine.

"You don't know that," she sobbed into him, her hands wrapped around his middle.

He felt them shake.

"I can take care of myself, Sugar."

Marta wiggled out of his embrace, looking at him with an unreadable expression.

"What did you just call me?"

"Sugar. Not okay?"

"No, well yes. I don't know. I like it."

They looked at each other before bursting into laughter. That was the most confusing answer she had ever given him.

"Sugar it is then."

He pulled her in for another hug, knowing that she needed him close now.

"You won't lose me, Sugar. I promise," he added.

"I didn't expect to lose Frank either. He was a lawyer, Oliver. I was the Agent, the one out in the field, undercover. He was a fucking lawyer. I brought that criminal into our house. I got him killed. He was innocent."

Her sobs were heartbreaking for Oliver and all he wanted to do was bring her some comfort, but he couldn't. Instead he carefully guided her towards the couch again, sitting down and placing her on his lap, straddling him. He still held her close, comforting her as best as he could while she finally let go of all the emotions she'd been holding back for a very long time.

Probably since Frank died.

"I know, Sugar, but it wasn't your fault. The mafioso followed you, broke into your house, and hurt him. There's nothing you could've done to prevent this."

"But what if..."

"No. No what if's. You did your job, that's all. It is *not* your fault."

He placed a shy kiss on her forehead, making her furrow her brow at the unexpected intimacy.

"I just... I just can't lose you, too. I wouldn't be able to survive it again."

"You don't have to. I won't get killed."

"But you're a CIA Agent, going on operations all the time. All the time, Oliver. I can't sit back home in my office feeling my stomach turn because I'm terrified something could happen to you. That would be agonizing. Also, I'm your boss, I command you on those missions. You think I could make the right decisions if we were romantically involved?"

"*Romantically involved*. Wow. That phrase is a big meh," Oliver groaned.

"Oliver," Marta sighed.

"Sorry, Sugar. You're the best Deputy Director of Operations that I've ever met and even though Gary from HR doesn't share that opinion with me, I am 100% convinced that you'd always make the right decision."

"But what if I had to choose between you and Butch? Who do we bring back home in case both of you are critically hurt and we only have one medical team? How could I make that decision without letting our relationship or my fear of losing you influence it?"

There were so many absurd scenarios in her head. She'd thought this through so many times. Each time she tried to convince herself to give him a chance. That she was ready. That it was going to be okay. Frank had been her ultimate excuse to say no to him in the end. Every damn time.

"You and I both know that that's a very unrealistic scenario and even if you find yourself in that situation, you won't have to make the decision alone. Director Burns will always help you. You won't let our relationship destroy your job. You just won't, Marta."

She wanted to believe him so badly but something inside of her was still holding her back.

"I can't have kids," she blurted out.

Another reason she had declined his dates. Oliver wanted kids and he was so good with them. Frequently over the years they'd visited schools around Washington, explaining to kids and teenagers what CIA Agents do and how they would be able to join. Oliver always wanted to go to the primary schools, his face lighting up as soon as he saw the kids running around on the playground. He'd be a great dad someday.

Marta leaned back, scanning his face for any kind of reaction to her words. She saw sadness in the depths of his eyes and he was unable to hide it.

"Oh," he whispered, his façade now falling completely.

"One of my ovaries was hit by the bullet, so they had to cut it out."

"And the other one?"

"Is still in me."

"So technically you can have kids?" His eyes widened, hope filling his voice.

"Technically yes, but it is very unlikely. The doctors said it would take a lot of patience and I shouldn't risk it too many times."

"That's enough for me," he said and placed another kiss on her forehead.

"Oliver..."

"No, Marta. I understand your concerns and your fears. I really do. I know it's not exactly the same but I still feel like that with Butch. When we went on the first operation together after he started at the CIA, I watched him more than I should, losing focus on the target and letting the terrorist flee. It became better over time, but I still have a bad gut feeling when we're heading towards Iraq," he sighed loudly, the memories of what had happened to his best friend Nate flashing through his mind.

"Then you understand why I can't date you. I'm not ready for this."

Oliver couldn't hide his disappointment and sadness, but he grabbed her face with both of his hands.

"I understand. One day you will, I know it and I'll ask you over and over again until you finally say yes. I promise you."

Marta chuckled, imagining Oliver asking her every single day. She wasn't completely wrong, although he only asked her once a week from that day forward.

"I hope you know that you're the best," she whispered, leaning herself against him for another hug.

"Doing the best I can," he chuckled a little.

"Does this change anything between us?" She asked, scared.

"Not at all, Sugar. You can't get rid of me that easily. I'd be very depressed if I couldn't have dinner and movie nights with you anymore."

"Or get yourself destroyed in Cluedo," she added.

"Yeah, or that."

Both of them started to laugh before Oliver let her go from his hug.

"I'm still your best friend but one day I'll be your boyfriend. That's the official warning."

"Yeah. One day."

SECRECY

NOW

July 31st, 2022

"Come on, *mi cielo*. You need to wake up. We have to make breakfast," Marta whispered in Oliver's ear before placing a few kisses along his jaw.

"Why did we decide to do this again?" Oliver sighed, refusing to open his eyes as he turned around and pulled the blanket over his head.

Marta chuckled, trying to free his head from the blanket but Oliver held fast against her. He was way stronger so Marta didn't stand a chance. She chuckled again, trying to tickle his waist through the blanket, but it didn't bother him.

"Come ooooonnnn. It's Lynn's 30th birthday. We need to do something special," Marta complained, trying to convince Oliver in an emotional way.

"She has a boyfriend for that. Why is Butch not making her breakfast?" Oliver's voice came from under the blanket. He was still hiding.

Before Marta could answer him they heard a loud moan from the room next door. In an instant Oliver appeared from under the blanket, looking wide-eyed at Marta. The Deputy Director burst into laughter while Oliver jumped out of the bed. He was only in his boxers, looking for the clothes he had spread around the room the night before. He hurried to get into them while mumbling "Oh gosh, I do *not* want to hear that" over and over again. With one leg already in his sweatpants he jumped around the room in a desperate attempt to not lose his balance. After struggling for several seconds he finally managed to get the second leg into his pants so he was finally ready to flee.

Marta couldn't stop laughing, lying on her side, holding her stomach. The panicking Oliver, who was getting more and more frantic with the ongoing moans from the room next door, was a hilarious thing to observe.

When the blond Agent was fully clothed, he looked at Marta in expectation.

"Come on, Sugar. There's breakfast to prepare."

"Yeah, I bet they need some fuel after their morning workout."

"Maaaaarrttaaaaaaa," Oliver whined, storming out of the room with his face furrowed in a grimace.

She was still laughing as she rolled out of bed and put on her own clothes before following Oliver into the community kitchen.

Together they started preparing different kinds of breakfast dishes. Thankfully Tia and Birdie joined after a while, helping them with the tremendous amount of food they wanted to make.

Over the last few weeks Marta had contacted the few people in Lynn's life who were not living at headquarters.

Toby hadn't been around in a while as he'd gotten a promotion at the hospital he worked at. He was now leading a team of five young doctors and was responsible for their education and specializations, but for Lynn's 30th birthday he'd taken a day of his PTO to make sure that no emergency would stop him from coming.

Oliver had also asked their colleagues Jakob and Peter if they'd come around for breakfast. It was a Sunday and, as both of them were living away from headquarters, he wanted to make sure they'd be okay. Of course they agreed.

Marta's last idea was to invite Lynn's parents but as she knew that there was an uncomfortable silence within the family she wasn't sure if she should do it. Oliver and she had a long conversation about it and agreed that this could be a turning point for the family. The risk was high and to be completely sure that they would make the right decision, Oliver even consulted Nate to ask for his opinion.

Lynn's boyfriend agreed with them that they should give it a try and invite Thea and Jensen. It could go either way. Lynn could hate them for inviting her parents and it could ruin the mood and they would have to endure a very uncomfortable breakfast, or they would take the chance to forgive each other.

While Oliver, Marta, Birdie, and Tia prepared every item for the breakfast, more and more people appeared and helped them decorate or cook. Jakob's wife Maja had given him two boxes full of birthday decorations that they had left from their son's birthday. They contained a garland that spelled 'Happy Birthday' in golden letters, confetti, and other decorations for the big table as well as one confetti cannon.

"We can use it to surprise her," Jakob suggested with a wide grin on his face.

He was known as the clown among his colleagues, always having a joke on his lips, laughing more often than being serious. Lynn and he shared a weird sense of humor, as both of them were fans of dad jokes and anti-jokes.

For once Marta agreed with Jakob, thinking that surprising Lynn with a confetti cannon could actually be funny for everybody.

Peter brought two big balloons that showed a '30' and they placed them along the wall behind the dinner table.

Everything looked perfect, the food was done, and they were right on time. All they needed to do was wait for Lynn.

Around twenty minutes later they heard noises coming from the hallway so everybody tried to be as quiet as possible. Marta had the confetti cannon in her hands, waiting for Lynn to walk through the door.

The moment the doctor did, Marta covered her in colorful confetti while most of the others just started to laugh.

Lynn was surprised at the sudden outburst. She was tired, she was sore, and all she did was turn around to bury her face in Nate's chest. Oliver looked at his best friend with furrowed eyebrows, scared that the confetti cannon would trigger him but, instead of looking into a scared face like Oliver had for the last ten years, he watched Nate burst into laughter while gently patting Lynn's back.

Oliver's heart skipped a beat and the lingering weight of guilt and sadness on his shoulders disappeared.

Nate was okay. His best friend was okay. After more than a decade of fighting against the demons in his mind, Oliver finally watched Nate laugh and smile with the woman he had fallen in love with.

Instinctively Oliver's eyes wandered to Marta, the woman he himself had fallen in love with and who was finally his girlfriend.

She stood a few feet in front of him, her honey-colored eyes decorated by wrinkles while she smiled widely. Although they'd been up pretty early you couldn't see any exhaustion on her pretty face. Her cheeks slightly red from rushing around and preparing everything, her beautiful lips curled into an infectious smile and that one strand of hair that had fallen from behind her ear, framing her face perfectly.

She was the most beautiful woman Oliver had ever seen and he felt his lips turn upward as well. How could he be so lucky to have this woman as his girlfriend?

He felt the immense urge to step next to her, grab her by the waist, and pull her into a fierce kiss but he couldn't because their relationship was still a secret. Marta was Oliver's boss and the CIA's policy about relationships between work colleagues was very strict.

They had seen Lynn and Nate talking to HR about their relationship, being interviewed for hours to make sure that their love wouldn't affect their work. In the end, HR thankfully didn't give them any consequences but they were still under observation.

Oliver and Marta would never get that allowance from HR, which would lead to one of them changing their job. Maybe within the Agency, maybe even outside. That was something they didn't want to face yet. Maybe one day, when their relationship was settled enough.

After the initial shock, Lynn thanked Oliver and Marta for preparing the breakfast surprise before she started an uncomfortable conversation with her parents.

They'd been very quiet since they arrived and both Marta and Oliver had an inkling in their stomachs that inviting them probably wasn't the best idea, especially as Lynn's father Jensen was even more grumpy than Butch at his worst.

Everyone could sense the growing tension so Marta's voice was a welcome distraction from the rumbling family drama.

"Breakfast is served. Everybody, please take a seat."

The table was filled with all the delicious breakfast dishes Oliver and Marta had made earlier that morning: pancakes, waffles, French toast, a big bowl of oatmeal, and even hearty dishes like scrambled eggs and different variations of sandwiches.

"This looks amazing. When did you prepare all this?" Lynn asked surprised, her head turned towards Marta and Oliver.

"We were up pretty early. Couldn't sleep anyways..." Oliver answered while throwing a knowing glance between Nate and Lynn.

The doctor blushed immediately and scrunched her face in shame. Oliver and Marta burst into laughter and Toby followed after realizing what Oliver meant.

The fact that only Lynn and Nate knew about their relationship, didn't stop them from having as much physical contact as possible. Oliver had his legs parted, his right knee pressing against Marta's left the entire time but that wasn't enough for him. He tried to test the limits around their friends so he had his right hand placed on Marta's thigh while they ate breakfast.

His thumb brushed over the thick fabric of her jeans and goosebumps appeared everywhere he touched her. She was scared the others would realize what was going on as Oliver was right-handed and was forced to eat with his left hand so he could touch her. The adrenaline rushing through Marta's veins made her heart beat faster.

It felt like a rush, both terrifying and exhilarating.

When Oliver leaned back in his seat after finishing breakfast she could see the bulge in his way too tight jeans. The ones he was wearing already emphasized his crotch but the adrenaline of getting caught had turned him on, making the bulge more present than usual. Marta was surprised but she tested the limits even further when she leaned over the table to grab another waffle. Her head was near his ears when she whispered:

"I'll take care of you later."

She could see him stifle the groan that almost escaped his throat and he quickly jumped to his feet, grabbed his coffee mug, and almost ran to the kitchen island. He pressed some buttons on the coffee machine to get a refill while his eyes were fixed on Marta's. Marta turned her head to see everybody busy in discussions about coffee specialties before she winked at Oliver. The blond Agent smirked at her and grabbed his crotch to rearrange whatever was going on beneath his jeans. Marta couldn't wait to peel the tight fabric off his muscular thighs later.

When everybody was done eating they stored the leftovers in the fridge and scattered into smaller groups for small talk. Marta had approached Oliver to enjoy some conversation with him but the young Agent Peter Davis was quicker and started to talk to her boyfriend.

"Have you tried the new simulations after the update?" Peter asked, his eyes wide and full of sparkles.

Marta didn't know what they were talking about, but Peter's passion for the topic was clearly visible.

"Not yet. Too much going on at the moment." Oliver smiled back at the young man.

Marta could see his smile, but it didn't reach his eyes. He was always polite, but whatever topic Peter had chosen for their conversation, Oliver was not interested at all.

"What are you two talking about?" Marta asked, stepping next to Oliver and bumping her shoulder into his.

He turned his head towards her and gave her a smile, a real one this time. She could practically see the hearts flying out of it. That man was head over heels for her, and she felt her cheeks burning when he looked at her like this. Peter didn't seem to notice, as he continued the conversation like no magic moment between Marta and Oliver had happened at all:

"Our VR shooting range got an update last week and we have more simulations available now."

"Oh, that's cool. Haven't used that range in months," Marta spoke and felt Oliver's hand carefully lingering over the small of her back.

There was only the wall with the television behind them so nobody could see his bold movement.

"We could do a mission together. That would be fun," Oliver said, his hand wandering down to Marta's butt.

"Yes, you'd be a great team," Peter commented.

"Agreed. We never worked together while I was still an Agent so we could use the simulation to see how we would work out in the field."

Marta had her head still turned to Oliver, looking deep into his green-blue eyes. His hand was completely covering one of her butt cheeks and instead of answering her verbally, he squeezed it.

Marta cleared her throat to hide the squeaking sound that almost slipped through her lips and turned her head towards Peter. The young, naive Agent looked at her with a wide grin still on his face, unable to recognize what happened in front of him or that he was third-wheeling the secret couple.

"Let me know, I wanna see that. Heard a lot of stories about your time as active Agent, Marta." Peter smiled at her.

"You did?"

"Yeah, Liam and I like to work out together and he told me a lot about your missions."

"Liam? Liam Thomas?" Marta's eyes widened and she looked at Peter in shock.

"Yeah. I didn't know he knew so much about you, but his stories are impressive."

"Well, Peter…" Oliver started, his hand leaving Marta's butt to place it on Peter's shoulder instead.

The young Agent looked at his team leader in surprise.

"You know that Liam and Marta never worked together, right?"

Peter's eyes alternated between Oliver and Marta, the processing in his brain clearly visible in his facial expression. He was like a younger brother to Oliver, as he tried to make a good Agent and man out of him. Peter was like a raw diamond that needed some time, love, and pressure to form him into the perfect Agent. But Oliver had seen his potential right from the beginning.

"I… I didn't know that. But how does he…"

Peter's eyes widened in shock, and his lips parted when he realized how Liam had all this information.

Liam Thomas was a hacker who the CIA had hired a few months ago. He'd operated from his apartment for over a decade while officially working as an accountant. Oliver first had contact with him when Liam gave the Navy SEALs the location of the hideout where a terrorist held Nate captive. Thanks to Liam they were able to save Nate. Earlier this year Liam helped the CIA to find William Taylor, who worked as a broker between mafias and terrorists, setting up deals about weapons. Liam was one of the best hackers in the world, a fact he was really aware of and told everybody he met.

Neither Marta nor Oliver knew that Peter and Liam spent time together in their free time so Marta didn't know that Liam used his hacking skills to get into the reports of her operations back in the day. They weren't highly confidential, but they also weren't easy to find.

"It's okay, Peter. I'll have a word with Liam tomorrow." Marta winked at the young Agent, who nodded in agreement.

He looked still pretty shocked, with a blush of shame on his face before he excused himself to use the restrooms.

Finally Marta and Oliver were alone... well at least as alone as you can be in a room full of people. They looked around and saw most of their friends in conversations. Only Lynn and her father were missing and Marta wondered where they had gone. Nate was standing awkwardly next to Lynn's mom Thea, trying to have a conversation with her but even when his mental recovery was going amazing he still had problems with people he'd never met before. His eyes frantically scanned the room while Thea silently took a sip of her coffee. Oliver's best-friend-instinct kicked in and he wanted to save Nate, but the moment he started moving, Marta linked her pinky finger with his. He immediately stopped in his tracks and fixed his eyes on his girlfriend. Her back shielded their linked hands from the curious looks of people in the room but it was still risky. They had tested their luck multiple times today and it was only a matter of time before someone caught them.

"We need to be more careful," Oliver whispered toward Marta.

He could see the sadness in her eyes when she let go of his finger and stepped back to get some distance between them.

"You're right. My hormones are making me do dumb stuff today."

"Your hormones?"

"Yeah. Your tight jeans are driving me crazy," she sighed exaggeratedly, carefully pointing at Oliver's crotch.

"Why are they driving you crazy?"

"Because it's like you're holding your dick right in my face, but I can't have it."

Marta's voice was so low that Oliver almost missed her words.

"You can have it."

"But not right now."

Her eyes portrayed the sadness that he could hear in her voice.

Now they were finally in a relationship, they hadn't been able to keep their hands off each other and they had sex at every opportunity. Oliver fought hard to finally be able to be with her and he wouldn't waste another second.

"I'm gonna go to the men's restroom. You can follow me in a minute."

"Oliver McGreen, what are you up to?"

"You'll see." He winked at her.

"You know that we have rooms here, right?"

"I know."

He stepped away from her and Marta shook her head with a smirk on her face. This man drove her crazy and she was enjoying every second of it.

She placed her coffee mug in the dishwasher and slowly stepped towards the door. On her right side she could see a beautiful reunion between Lynn and her parents, and it seemed like she and her dad finally took the chance to forget the happenings at the funeral. She was happy for Lynn but right now her brain was steered by lust and she needed to get to Oliver as soon as possible.

She stepped through the door and looked for him. Unlike most public restrooms, this one had cubicles with normal doors instead of the usual ones with gaps in. The door to the last room was wide open and she slowly stepped towards it.

Marta hadn't even made it a foot into the room when Oliver roughly grabbed her waist, pulled her towards him, and crashed his lips on hers. She kissed him back with the same passion and fire, extending her arm behind her to close the door.

"I've been wanting to do this the entire morning," he whispered on her lips before slowly nipping at them.

"You're such a bad boy."

"You love me like that."

"Fuck, yes," Marta groaned, pressing her hips tightly against the growing erection under Oliver's jeans.

He bucked his own hips in response, moaning slightly while fumbling with the lock of the door to make sure nobody could disturb them.

Oliver stripped off his shirt, knowing how much she loved to see his naked upper body. Marta let her finger follow the lines in his abs until she reached the waistband of his jeans. Her other hand tangled in Oliver's blond hair while they kissed each other again. It was almost impossible for her to open the buttons on Oliver's jeans one-handed but he moved his hips away anyway.

"You're not in charge this time, Sugar," he whispered before nipping her lip again to make her part her lips so he could slip his tongue into her mouth.

He was rough and needy and she loved it. The rare change of dynamic felt amazing. Marta already had wetness pooling between her thighs as the adrenaline of getting caught had kept her on edge the entire morning.

Oliver opened the buttons of his jeans and let them fall down to his ankles before he worked on

Marta's. Shuffling across the floor, he changed positions so that he stood with his back pressed against the door. Oliver grabbed Marta's jeans and pushed them down before he carefully took one leg after the other and freed her from the fabric. He repeated the same with her panties, before quickly stroking his finger along her core.

"You're already wet for me," he rasped, his pupils dilating as a wide grin spread over his face.

"You touching me the whole morning has that effect on me, *mi cielo*."

Oliver groaned in response, grabbing his hard cock through his boxers while crashing his lips on Marta's again.

"I'll show you what I;ve been wanting to do to you the entire morning," he whispered in between kisses, pulling her closer until her belly was pressed against his cock.

Marta reached one hand down, let it slip into his boxers, and grabbed his dick. She gave him a few strokes, seeing Oliver's head fall back and lean against the door. His eyes were closed while he enjoyed her fingers traveling up and down his shaft, applying the right amount of pressure to make him even more feral than before.

He'd imagined her hand on his cock the entire morning, spreading his legs extra wide while sitting at the breakfast table to give her a hint. Oliver knew that his jeans emphasized his cock through the fabric and he knew that she wouldn't be able to ignore it. Even after putting his dick on display during breakfast, she didn't get the hint but finally her perfect fingers were wrapped around his cock, exactly like they were meant to be.

But he needed more. He needed to be inside her.

Oliver grabbed her arm and felt Marta's fingers leave his cock. For a second he felt bad but then focused on pushing his boxers down to his ankles as well.

"I'm gonna fuck you now, Sugar," he rumbled, placing his hands underneath Marta's butt cheeks and lifting her body in the air.

He was strong, but he knew he wouldn't be able to hold her like that forever, so there was no time for fancy foreplay.

"Come one, *mi cielo*. Fill me up."

Marta had wrapped her arm around his neck to help him balance her body. Her face was pressed against his jaw and she gently nibbled along it while Oliver struggled to line his cock up with her entrance.

"Dammit," he mumbled after a few failed tries.

"What's wrong?"

"This looks way easier in movies than it is in real life. The angle is hard to find."

Marta reached down between them to give him a helping hand and finally he found the right angle to push inside of her. Both of them gasped and Marta buried her teeth in Oliver's neck to stifle another moan.

"I love you so much," he murmured while starting to move his hips to thrust into her over and over again.

Marta clenched on him tightly while every one of his thrusts made her brain more and more fuzzy. She wasn't able to think properly but thankfully she didn't need to. All that mattered was the two of them connected in the best possible way.

Oliver had the majority of work to do this time and with every thrust his back crashed against the door. A symphony of the vibrating door, slapping skin, and stifled moans filled the small room while they were chasing their highs together.

Suddenly they heard the door to the restrooms open and someone enter the room. The person was whistling while heading into the cubicle next to theirs.

Oliver stilled his movements, slightly panting from exertion, while Marta buried her face in his neck. She wasn't sure if she should freak out or start to laugh while they tried to be as silent as possible with Oliver still rock hard inside of her.

She could feel his arms starting to tremble under her weight and she knew that he wouldn't be able to hold her any longer.

Carefully she shifted her body a little and pointed with one hand on the toilet. As silently as possible, Oliver moved them around and closed the toilet so that he could sit on top of it. The lid crashed down on the seat and both of them stiffened. Now the person next to them must have known that there was someone else in the restroom as the sounds echoed around the small space.

Oliver slowly sat down on the toilet seat but slipped out of Marta as they moved. She extended her legs to stand on her own two feet while looking down at Oliver and his still hard cock.

They heard the toilet flush and the person heading out of the room and towards the sinks. A minute later the door to the restroom was heard again, indicating that they were finally alone.

With a smooth movement, Marta placed her hands on each of Oliver's shoulders and let herself lower down on his cock.

"Marta!" Oliver moaned while he felt her clench around him. They were both close and the unexpected visit catapulted them right to the edge. With her feet on the floor, Marta was perfectly able to bounce up and down on his cock in an intensity and speed like never before. It brought both of them the ultimate pleasure.

"I can't hold it any longer," Marta moaned and Oliver could already feel her clench around his cock.

The mixture of her moans, the pressure on his cock and the adrenaline in his body, let him spill deep inside of her with a graveled moan of her name.

They were both panting while Marta stilled her movement.

"Wow."

"Yeah, wow, Sugar. That was intense."

He smiled at her before leaning in to place a kiss on her lips.

"You think he heard us?" Marta laughed, knowing all too well that if the person had realized that Marta and Oliver were having sex in the bathroom it would cause them a lot of problems.

"Oh definitely. Let's hope it was Butch," Oliver laughed as well, both of them still riding the rest of their highs.

They were love drunk and couldn't assess the severity of them almost being caught properly.

"So much about our secret relationship," Marta sighed, rising to her feet.

She turned around to collect her clothes and hopped into them again. Oliver rose to his feet too, still completely naked, and pulled Marta towards him.

"It's gonna be okay. I promise."

He placed a kiss on her forehead, before getting into his own clothes.

They were enjoying the heat of the moment but he knew that Marta would regret it in a few minutes. It had been his idea because he'd been turning her on deliberately the entire morning but he didn't think about the risk of getting caught.

"I wish we didn't have to hide," she whispered toward the door.

Oliver placed his hand on her back while stepping towards her. His hand moved from her back to around her waist so that he could pull her against his chest.

"One day," he said before placing a loving kiss on the back of her head.

"Yeah, one day. I can't wait for it to come."

"Me neither."

CLUELESS

Then
December 24th, 2021

"I don't know what to do. I wish you were here to help me with this decision," Marta sighed deeply while standing in front of the cold grave.

Just as she did every year on this day, she visited Frank and Peach, brought them a bouquet of flowers, and talked to them.

Christmas was one of those holidays when the cemeteries were crowded with people because this holiday was made for families and on those days people miss their loved ones the most. More people in the cemetery meant more people around her who could see and hear her talk to a freaking stone. Although it was common in books and movies, in reality not many people actually spoke to the bodies lying within the graves. Marta did and she didn't care if people thought she was crazy. It was her ritual to tell Frank about the past year, about every milestone she had reached after he was ripped out of her life, and about the good and the bad things that had happened to her.

This year was the same as usual; Marta stood in front of the grave, her arms crossed in front of her chest to press the fabric of her winter coat even closer to her freezing body. It was unusually cold today, mainly due to a freezing breeze that forced Marta to wear a beanie. She hated any kind of hat, but Oliver had insisted that she would freeze to death if she didn't wear it. Of course she didn't own a beanie, so Oliver gave her his navy blue one that had the SEAL's logo on the front. It was a little big for her head so she had to readjust it every few minutes or the wool would cover her eyes completely.

"I feel stupid for coming here and asking you for help regarding love. This feels so wrong."

She started to pace up and down along Frank's grave, her heart suddenly weighing a ton. Every heartbeat was heavy within her chest while guilt crawled through her entire nervous system. What a stupid idea to go to her dead husband's grave to talk about someone she may or may not have fallen in love with.

A stronger breeze swelled, almost brushing the wide beanie off Marta's head. She quickly grabbed it with one of her hands while the other was occupied getting the strands of hair out of her face.

"I hate this weather. I know Christmas was always your favorite holiday but the cold is something I'll never get used to. I miss snuggling in your arms under the big red blanket on our couch. You were even cuddlier after we found out about Peach. Not that I dared to complain, I enjoyed it a lot."

A smile crept across her face as she thought about them cuddling in their house. It had been a magical time when the Peach was a secret between the two of them. Frank's hand landed on her barely visible pregnancy belly as soon as they were in the same room. He would have been an amazing dad.

But some assholes took him and Peach away from her and now she was forced to go to their graves to talk to them. Frank had been the best listener, shooting some random answers or questions here and there but mostly being patient and letting her ramble. About her friends, her family, or her job. No matter what the topic was, he listened.

People she clicked with were very rare in her life and as soon as she found someone, she held onto them and refused to let them out of her life.

Oliver was one of those people and she was happy that he'd found his way into her life. He'd been by her side when she'd needed a friend and hadn't left since. Although their connection was pretty deep right from the beginning Marta knew that she would have the same connection to him if she had met him without her trauma. They would have been good friends anyway but then, obviously, she would've never thought about falling in love with him.

"I like him, you know. He's sweet and caring, and he makes me laugh every day. We started buying each other ugly mugs whenever we saw one. You'd love them, they're hilarious."

Marta let out a loud chuckle while thinking about one particular mug that was shaped like the head of a bear and looked hilarious but was impossible to drink out of. She'd just found a white mug with the outline of a fist on one side that said "I'm the boss. Listen to me or I'll throw this mug at you" printed on it. It would be her Christmas present for Oliver this year. Marta couldn't stop smiling as she imagined the Agent opening the package and seeing the mug for the first time.

Marta shook her head in defeat because even while standing in front of her husband's grave, all she could think about was Oliver. Had infectious laughter in her ears when she imagined him seeing the newest mug to their collection.

Another cold, but stronger breeze brushed the oversized beanie off her head and blew multiple strands of hair over her face. She gasped while trying to get rid of the hair with hasty movements of her hands.

"That damn wind," she mumbled when she was finally able to see again.

Marta kneeled down to pick up Oliver's navy-blue beanie and let it rest in her hands. It smelled like him, and she couldn't deny that she loved his woody scent, which smelled like a forest early in the morning. It always calmed her and brought her peace. Her thumbs were gently rubbing over the material, while another smile appeared on her face.

"I miss you, baby. Christmas isn't the same without you, although Oliver tries his best to entertain me. This year was especially exhausting. He forced me to bake Christmas cookies four times as well as build gingerbread houses together with Butch. You should have seen Butch's. He basically coated it in icing so that the whole house was just white. Then he placed some smarties on it, before crushing it again and starting to eat it right away. Oliver's face was hilarious when he gave Butch a ten-minute speech about why you shouldn't eat the entire gingerbread house while still making it. I'm pretty sure he made half of the stuff up, like you'd have bad sex for the next five years. Never heard someone being so upset about something so irrelevant. I couldn't stop laughing, so Oliver decided to smear icing all over my face because I didn't support him in his rant. Butch was completely overwhelmed by the situation and just fled. That lucky bastard, I had to deal with a grumbling Oliver for two more hours," Marta chuckled a little, seeing the scene right in front of her eyes.

"You would've been a great addition to the chaos, Baby. You and Oliver would've been great friends. Anyway, I'm talking about him again the whole time."

She ended her monologue with a loud sigh, her heart heavy again as guilt started to creep into her body.

Before she could actually tell Frank about something else, an unexpected breeze brought some chaos into her hair, letting them fly around before settling down anywhere but where they were supposed to.

"What's with that damn wind? There wasn't a single breeze over the last few minutes. Holy shit."

Marta struggled to get her hair back in place with a few groans of annoyance.

"You'd laugh at me like you always did."

A memory of them walking along the coastline came to her mind. It had been very windy that day and Marta was not wearing a beanie, hat, or anything else that would have been able to tame her hair. Instead they were flying around the entire time while she was cussing the hell out of them. Frank had stopped eventually, doubling over, and couldn't stop laughing. It was like this laughter was still in her ears when she brought her attention back to the graveyard.

Instead of hearing any kind of answer, another breeze destroyed her just sorted hair again.

"Son of a bitch," she hissed, but more and more breezes came up, making it impossible for her to not look like an old crow in the wind.

Her curly hair was always a mess, but with enough time, patience, and a lot of hair products she was able to look acceptable every day. But this stupid wind decided to ruin her good hair day today and that made her furious. Marta stomped on the floor, her hands buzzing around to catch some of the strands and push them out of her face while she groaned over and over again.

The trees around her were howling and it sounded like they were laughing at her. For a brief second, she thought she could hear Frank's laughter again and her eyes widened.

"You think this is funny?" she asked the grave and another strong breeze came up but this time she was prepared, holding most of her hair down and out of her face.

"Don't pull this *Mufasa Lion King* shit with me, Frank."

Another breeze, another howling of the trees.

Her heartbeat quickened drastically, and she suddenly felt dizzy. Could this be true? Could Frank communicate with her through the wind?

Marta shook her head. She was the Deputy Director of the CIA, she did not believe in any kind of hocus-pocus.

"I don't know what I should do with him, Frank. I like him, but I shouldn't. You're my husband and I don't want to have feelings for any other man but you. I promised you my eternal love and I don't plan on breaking that promise."

She sighed loudly again, tears brimming in her eyes.

"But he really makes me happy and the more time we spend together and he asks me for a date, the more my heart aches to say yes to him. I feel like I need to convince myself more and more that we're just friends. That it wouldn't be right to be more. Because it wouldn't, right?"

She looked at the grave, silently waiting for another breeze to come up as a reaction from Frank. Great, now she was going insane because of the weird coincidence of a series of breezes. Marta let out a long breath, unable to hide the slight pain of disappointment in her chest. She really needed her husband for a real conversation.

"Of course *now* you're silent. Now, when I really need your help. I don't even know why I asked for your opinion when it's crystal clear that I should never date him."

The strongest breeze so far began to blow, making Marta lose her balance and she had to step back and engage her core so as to not fall to the ground.

"What the hell?! Are you disagreeing with me, or what? I *should* date him?" She almost spit at the grave, annoyance taking the best of her.

Within a few seconds a cloud moved past the sun and the sunlight reached her skin making heat slowly seep back into every cell of skin that it illuminated.

"You gotta be freaking kidding me," Marta chuckled under her breath, not quite able to believe what just happened. The breezes would have been easy to explain, but the sudden appearance of the sun?

"Nobody will ever believe what just happened but let's be honest, I won't tell anyone anyway. They'd think I'm fucking crazy."

Her eyebrows were furrowed, and she looked at Frank's name on the grave with a scowl on her face.

"So you want me to date him, huh? Okay, but if it turns out to be a bad idea it's all your fault and I won't bring you flowers for a whole month."

Marta walked towards the inscription before kneeling and placing a kiss on every single letter. With a ceaseless smile on her lips she walked to her car to drive back home. *Home*. The CIA headquarters that had slowly but steadily become her home over the last few years and where Oliver really did his best to make her feel safe and comfortable.

Yes, she might give him a chance for a date. But not right away. He'd need to fight for it and one day, she'd say yes.

Her heart fluttered at the thought of going on a real and official date with him and in that moment, she was thankful that Frank forced her to make this decision.

It felt like the right one.

ONE DAY

NOW
December 23rd, 2023

"Sugar, would you bring me some marshmallows for my hot chocolate?" Oliver grabbed Marta's wrist as she was about to head towards the kitchen area of the community kitchen.

Today was their internal Christmas party and a lot of colleagues from all the different task forces had gathered around and decorated Christmas cookies. Marta had organized the festivities this year to connect people in the different task forces she was responsible for. They'd never had big corporate-wide events other than a summer barbecue, but that was for the whole CIA, so they didn't have the chance to converse between the task forces that were under the same Deputy Director. The terrorism task force and the drug trafficking task force had several operations together and for cases like that Marta wanted their teams to know each other.

That's why she and Oliver had organized this Christmas party together. They drank hot chocolate (with or without alcohol in it), listened to Christmas music, and decorated and ate cookies as well as a huge gingerbread house that Oliver had built with Nate.

To Marta's surprise the former Grinch had grown into a Christmas-loving guy, willingly baking and decorating a huge gingerbread house the size of a washing machine. Nate had been whistling and humming in the kitchen the whole of the previous day, decorating the walls and roofs with different colored icing as well as a wide variety of gummy stuff. Oliver had bought everything but not even he had thought Nate would have so much fun making the house.

To stick with their own tradition, Oliver and Marta were wearing ugly Christmas sweaters and, although they had a little collection after all these years, today they decided to appear at their Christmas party in the first set they ever got. The ones that Oliver bought for them in 2019.

"No probllama," Marta answered her boyfriend, referring to her own sweater.

Oliver burst into laughter and the Agents around him did as well. Instead of finally letting her go, Oliver pulled Marta closer again, his eyes looking at her with expectation. She knew exactly what he was up to, so she leaned down and placed a tender kiss on his lips. Oliver smiled into the kiss before he finally let her go, so she could get herself a new hot chocolate and marshmallows.

They had officially announced their relationship around Christmas last year after having multiple conversations with HR and even Director Burns. It wasn't easy and HR gave them a hard time. The original idea was that Marta wouldn't be responsible for the terrorism task force anymore but Director Burns vetoed that idea. The team trusted Marta and, after so many failed missions over the past year, he didn't want to demotivate them even further by changing their boss.

Firing one of them was off the table right away, as was forcing Oliver to change task forces. All of the regular solutions for this issue wouldn't work for Oliver and Marta and HR were not amused.

The final solution was strict supervision of each and every one of Marta's decisions regarding the terrorism task force, at least if it involved Oliver. She needed to write way more detailed protocols about the operations and the reasons for her decision so that HR could check if she were favoring Oliver in any way. It was super annoying and additional work, but Marta was willing to do it as long as she was finally able to behave freely around people other than their closest friends. Now they could hold hands or kiss each other whenever they wanted, without checking their backs the entire time. It was more than freeing.

Oliver had talked to Nate a lot about this topic, as he and Lynn had officially come out as a couple a while before. Things between his best friend and Lynn had even improved after they weren't forced to make a secret out of everything.

Well at least until their relationship had taken a different turn late 2022, but that was another story.

Marta stepped towards the kitchen island where she'd prepared a big pot of hot chocolate with a golden ladle in it to refill the mugs easily. It hadn't been one of the premade chocolates that only needed to be heated, but one made from scratch. You think it's only milk and chocolate? Not when you make a hot chocolate using Marta's special recipe. She used unsweetened cocoa powder, sweetened it with brown sugar and added a chopped chocolate bar into the hot milk. This combination always gave the best chocolatey taste, and she got compliments from everyone who tried a sip. Her secret ingredient was just a quarter teaspoon of vanilla extract as the vanilla helped to enhance the special taste of the chocolate milk.

Jakob was standing in front of the pot, currently refilling his mug, before grabbing the bottle of Liqueur 43 to pour into it as well. The combination of hot chocolate and liquor was something Marta saw as a family tradition as her whole family loved to drink it. It was the Gómez version of the Spanish specialty "Lumumba" that her parents had learned to love while they were still living in Spain. Although they had become very American over the years, Lumumba was something they tried to keep, even if it were a slightly different version.

To show her colleagues a bit of her culture she explained to them the story of the drink's name. Patrice Lumumba was a revolutionist and helped the Republic of the Congo get their independence in 1960. Unfortunately it's not really known why the Spanish decided to name the drink after Lumumba.

"This is so good, Marta. I don't think I'll ever drink normal hot chocolate again." Jakob smiled at her, his eyes slightly glassy from the multiple mugs he had already drunk over the afternoon.

He had his wife Maja and their two kids with him, who were occupied with decorating cookies of all shapes and sizes.

"Glad you like it, and happy that Maja is with you to drive you home. Wouldn't let you near a car in that state," Marta chuckled a little as well.

She hadn't drunk alcohol today as she was still the Deputy Director of all these Agents. It probably wouldn't have been a problem if she'd had a mug or two but she didn't want to. She wanted to make sure everything was going okay and that everybody enjoyed the afternoon and had everything they needed. That's why her main task today had been running around and bringing people stuff. New icing, new cookies, a refill of their mugs, or marshmallows for Oliver.

Speaking of Oliver...

The Agent had become a little impatient, seeing Marta chat with Jakob instead of bringing him his marshmallows. His chocolate was starting to get cold and he loved it when at least half the marshmallows melted and sweetened the chocolate even more than it already was. After years of getting these special hot chocolates from Marta he was used to perfection so he really needed the marshmallows now.

Approaching Marta he gently placed his hand on top of her butt, carefully looking around him so that nobody was watching them directly. Yes their relationship wasn't a secret anymore but they still didn't want to be too apparent about their love in front of their colleagues. Oliver turned his body in such a way that nobody at the dinner table was able to see where his hand had landed before he gently squeezed Marta's butt cheek. The Deputy Director squeaked a little, trying to hide Oliver's stealth attack in front of Jakob who was standing on the other side of the kitchen island. Close enough to realize that

Oliver had done something to make Marta react that way, but also too far away to see his hand. He was also slightly tipsy, making his brain take a little longer to process the couple's actions.

"I'll give you a minute," he mumbled before heading back towards Maja and the kids to check how many cookies they had already finished.

Oliver leaned into Marta to place a kiss on her cheek, his hand still grabbing perfectly around her butt cheek.

"I miss the secrecy," he whispered in her ear. "The adrenaline of getting caught always turned me on."

His voice made the Deputy Director blush the deepest red.

"We might not need to hide anymore, but I hope I still manage to turn you on, *mi cielo*."

"That you do, Sugar."

He dropped another kiss on her temple before grabbing the big bag of marshmallows and jogging back to his spot at the dinner table.

If someone had told her a few years ago that, after Frank's death and the loss of their unborn child, she would be happy again she wouldn't have believed it.

But slowly, steadily Oliver forced himself into her life, giving her the right support to let her heal the cracks in her heart. She'd never forget her past life because it had made her the person she was now but Marta had learned that, at some point, she had to move on. With the man who made her smile and laugh, who made her feel comfortable, safe and at home. He'd fought so hard to get that place in her heart and even after she'd refused him for so long, he'd kept on fighting.

And today Marta was more than grateful for that.

Grateful that Oliver not only accepted her rejection but also gave her all the time she needed to finally realize that he was the person she wanted to be with. He'd been by her side over the last few years, as a colleague, as a friend, and as a lover.

It was rare to find your best friend and partner in the same person, but she did. They'd overcome all the obstacles, all the doubts, and all the fears until they were finally carefree.

When Marta told him that one day she hoped they'd be able to not hide anymore, she didn't expect how good it would feel to show the world that this man belonged to her. That she'd won the grand prize, won the lottery. His heart was big enough for both of them and with every kiss and touch, he repaired her broken heart until it was healed again. And from that day on it only beat for him.

Marta smiled at the blond Agent sitting at the table, who was chatting with some colleagues from the drug trafficking task force. They were talking, smiling, and laughing about something she didn't understand. When Oliver turned his head slightly and his green-blue eyes met her honey-colored ones, Marta knew that he was everything she needed in her life. And that she would never let him go again.

Marta & Oliver will appear again in *Demons in your heart*!

MESSAGE

Sometimes good things need time.
But it's worth fighting for your happiness.
Don't give up so easily.

ACKNOWLEDGMENTS

Happy Birthday, **Marta**.

You were the first one to come up with the idea of telling the story of Oliver and the character that was named after you. Thank you for giving her your name and your face.

This novella and this fictional boyfriend is my birthday present for you. Never thought that this would be published. I feel like this story brought us even closer together than our favorite other topic. The character Marta is *not* you, but she has some of your characteristics and I like how she turned out. And obviously the sweet and caring Oliver that won your heart after chapter two. I am still in shock how that happened and how fast you let Nate fall and loved Oli instead.

I take that as a compliment though.

Thank you for being there for me during this rollercoaster of a time with the divorce, the fear of losing my house, Nimbus, and my whole existence.

Te quiero.

Ann, my rock, my anchor, my best friend. I feel like I said it all to you already but it's important that you always know that I owe you so much. You reached out your hand and helped me out of my rabbit hole. You were there when I needed you the most. Special thanks for flying to Edinburgh with me and giving me this chance to finally visit the one city I always dreamed about. It was not only a trip to visit a beautiful city, but also to heal my heart and mind and it helped me a lot. Thank you for this.

Becks, you are the real magician here. It is unbelievable how you managed to turn my word vomit into functional sentences. I know you didn't always have an easy time with me, but editing with you was a delight. I've learned so much from you and your suggestions and finally started to believe that a weird German writing a book in English wasn't the worst idea in the world. Thank you!

Don & Mel Saladino, I will always thank you for what you did for me because you two are a huge influence on my recovery journey. I am improving physically and mentally because of you and I will forever be grateful for you and especially your words to me in Mexico.

Thank you to **Ana** for this wonderful cover, **Maja** for not only being my alpha reader but also the captain of my hype crew, **Mihaela** for always believing in me, even though you haven't read this book yet.

Thank you to every single human on my street team for the support, the nice words and shout-outs. I wouldn't have done it without you. Special thanks to **Jacky** and **Tracey** for pushing me without ever wanting anything in return. You're angels!

Shicara, you had to listen to me ranting about too many ridiculous things but still you were there whenever I asked for help and you inspired me so much with your creativity.

Thank you **Thea** for helping me with the logistics of IngramSpark and answering all my questions.

I am also thankful for the rest of the wonderful human beings at the **SugarClub**.

Additional Thank you to **Erica**, **Harry**, my sister **Annika** who is fucking getting married next year and made me believe that true love and soulmates do exist, **Paloma** and the **MorningCrew**.

Jess: over and out.
For now.

ABOUT THE AUTHOR

Jessica Girke is a 30-year-old German who loves to write Contemporary Romance books that include heavy topics like mental health issues.

Her structured job as financial analyst is a great contrast to the creativity that floods her brain while writing books and short stories.

In her free time she loves to cook, work out, read while lying in a hammock in her garden, have movie nights with her best friend, or cuddle her cat Nimbus.

 jess.loves.writing

 jessicagirke@gmail.com

www.ingramcontent.com/pod-product-compliance
Lightning Source LLC
La Vergne TN
LVHW091414190726
843491LV00006B/1428

* 9 7 8 3 9 8 2 5 7 7 6 0 9 *